The HISTORY *of* HELPLESS HARRY

When Harry could no longer see the coach, he turned about. In so doing, he discovered Miss Trowbridge looking at him closely, looking at him the way everybody always did, with a simpering, suffocating sympathy he loathed from the bottom of his heart.

"Time to go home, young master," said Miss Trowbridge sweetly, earnestly.

Master! Harry well knew that he didn't look like any master. Nor, he also knew, would she treat him remotely like one. She—the jail keeper—was only making fun.

Reluctantly, Harry crawled to the back of the wagon and stared out as they started to move. But right then he swore himself the most sacred of vows: He would show *her* who was master, and soon.

Little Free
Library

Take A
Book

Leave A
Book

The HISTORY *of* HELPLESS HARRY

TO WHICH IS ADDED A VARIETY
OF AMUSING AND ENTERTAINING
ADVENTURES

By

AVI

With Pictures By
PAUL O. ZELINSKY

A BEECH TREE PAPERBACK BOOK
NEW YORK

The songs sung by Jeremiah Skatch are from *Divine Songs Attempted in Easy Language for The Use of Children* by Isaac Watts, the most popular children's poet of the seventeenth, eighteenth, and nineteenth centuries.

———————————————

Library of Congress Cataloging in Publication Data
Avi, 1937– The history of Helpless Harry: to which is added a variety of amusing and entertaining adventures / by Avi; pictures by Paul O. Zelinsky. p. cm.
Summary: Eleven-year-old Harry's adventures, involving lies, attempted robbery, and the possibility of murder, begin when his parents go away and he is left in the care of a young woman.
[1. Robbers and outlaws—Fiction.] I. Zelinsky, Paul O., ill. II. Title.
III. Title: Helpless Harry.
PZ7.A953Hi 1995b [Fic]—dc20 94-26356 CIP AC
ISBN 0-688-05303-3 (pbk.)

3 5 7 9 10 8 6 4 2

Originally published in 1980 by Pantheon Books.
First Beech Tree edition, 1995.
Published by arrangement with the author.

FOR LEE HAYS

The History of HELPLESS HARRY

CHAPTER 1

IN WHICH WE BEGIN BY INTRODUCING A HERO
NAMED HARRY · A LOOK, TOO, AT HIS DIGNI-
FIED PARENTS · ALSO, A MOST IMPORTANT
QUESTION IS ASKED

I will begin my story by calling to your notice
Horatio Stockton Edgeworth—who wished very
much to be called Harry—sitting in the hayloft
over the cow's stall in the barn, a place he often
went when he wished to be alone. Since Harry
was expressly forbidden to go there, he found it a
particularly pleasing place to consider his misfor-
tunes. So it was that October morning in 1845.
Harry, considering his latest misfortune, was
wondering: What was he to do?

Eleven years of age, Harry had a smooth round
face, a face that always seemed to be poking out
from beneath a cap he never would take off. His
hands were mostly in trouser pockets. His feet
seemed to slip rather than step. And yes, he did
have dark, soft eyes and an appealing mouth, all
of which made many people consider him small,
hopeless, and helpless—a boy in constant need of
protection.

"Horatio! Horatio Stockton Edgeworth! Where

is that small boy?" called Mr. Edgeworth.

If Harry seemed small, Mr. Edgeworth, Harry's father, seemed large. That is, he was too big for his stiff starched shirt, too big for his jacket, and too big for the side whiskers that stuck out from his round face like the bare wings of a plucked chicken.

Harry, up in the hayrick, decided that he had best save his decision making for after breakfast. Reluctantly, he came out of the barn.

"There you are, dear boy!" exclaimed Mr. Edgeworth. "Breakfast! Then a surprise!"

Sudden joy lifted Harry's spirits. Perhaps, after all, he would *not* have to do anything.

Harry's mother was waiting in the kitchen. Whatever age Mrs. Edgeworth was, she wanted to be older. With plump cheeks and puckered lips, she stood there dressed in a black-and-red-striped silk dress with a high collar that made her head poke up like a tall mushroom. Though her head was crowned with ringlets, there was very little ring about her. She was the type that would rather sigh, when a smile would do.

Like many families of the day, the Edgeworths read the Bible before breakfast. They had read it through so many times that Harry was allowed to choose the part he wished to read himself.

So it was that morning. In his low, soft voice, under his parents' proud, moist eyes, Harry read a short verse. Then they ate, slowly and carefully. Throughout, Harry kept wondering about the surprise.

At last the table was clear. Mr. Edgeworth stood, cleared his throat, and began:

"Horatio Stockton Edgeworth, your devoted father and adoring mother are soon off on a journey. You, being small, delicate, ill-disposed to travel—in a word, helpless—shall remain at home. Miss Annie Trowbridge, the minister's ward, shall come to take care of you. This requires a small gift to attest to our abiding affection."

With a flourish Mr. Edgeworth brought forth a little book hardly bigger than Harry's hand. Holding it open for display, Harry read the title:

A KISS
FOR A BLOW
being
A Collection of Stories
For Children Showing Them
How to Prevent Quarreling.

Harry, wishing only that he was even allowed near other children, hid his disappointment. Mr. Edgeworth, instead of taking notice, took the pen his wife offered and on the blank front page of the book wrote:

To Our Precious Little Horatio
A gift from his loving father and mother,
Mr. and Mrs. Abraham Edgeworth
October 1, 1845 A.D.

"Now, Horatio," said Mrs. Edgeworth once the gift had been bestowed, "Miss Trowbridge will soon be here for a brief visit to learn her duties. I do hope I don't have to remind you that Miss Trowbridge is the minister's ward. Prepare yourself!"

Before he was out of the kitchen, Harry already hated Miss Trowbridge, hated her more than anyone else in the world.

Why?

I call to your attention the person put into prison because of an unfair law. Is he angry at the society that allowed the law? No! Is he angry at the judge who found him guilty? Hardly ever. At whom, then, is he angry? He is angry at the jailer who locks him in his cell!

So it was with Harry. His society, which is to say his mother and father, considered him helpless and insisted that he be protected. But it was Miss Trowbridge, you see, who was to be his jailer. For that alone Harry hated her. He truly did!

Thus the question: What could he do? And thus the answer: He would punish Miss Trowbridge.

There was no question about that!

CHAPTER 2

MISS ANNIE TROWBRIDGE ARRIVES · A GREAT SECRET IS OVERHEARD! · AND THE RESULTS OF THAT

Miss Annie Trowbridge arrived at the Edgeworths' home at the specified time. Fifteen years of age, she was not thought very young in the year 1845. After all, girls were considered women at sixteen. And before that age, if a girl wished to marry (and many of them did), she had to get permission from her father. That Miss Trowbridge could not do because she had no father or mother. An orphan, she was the ward of Dr. Williams, the minister. He had taken her into his house solely (so he said himself) out of a desire to protect her from a cruel world. That she cooked, cleaned, washed and took over all the other household duties for him was quite incidental. With such claims to respectability and hard work, it is easy

"Pleased to meet you, Horatio," said Miss Trowbridge . . .

to understand why Mrs. Edgeworth had chosen her to take care of Horatio.

"This," said Mrs. Edgeworth when the family received Miss Trowbridge, "is our darling boy, Horatio Stockton Edgeworth."

"Pleased to meet you, Horatio," said Miss Trowbridge with a bob.

Harry, standing polished and pickled, buffeted and bullied, scrubbed and scolded, dared not say what was in his mind. Instead, he kept his eyes focused on an ant struggling through a tiny crack in the wooden floor.

"Shy!" exclaimed Mrs. Edgeworth with a happy sigh.

"Helpless!" added Mr. Edgeworth.

Harry, pushing his foot forward, effectively crushed the ant with the hope that he could do the same to Miss Trowbridge.

"Shall we leave the ladies?" said Mr. Edgeworth to his son.

Harry, having no desire to remain with his father, quickly managed to get away. Whatever his outward appearance, he was very much interested in the young lady.

Eluding his father, he silently slipped back just outside the room where his mother was speaking to Miss Trowbridge. Making sure he could not be seen, but could hear everything, he stood quite still.

"There is one important thing," Mrs. Edgeworth was saying. "As you will have responsibility for the house you should be aware that Mr. Edgeworth keeps all his money beneath the floor board under his bed. You will find sufficient funds there when, and *if*, the need arises. Needless to say, there is a complete, entire accounting of its contents, and you shall be held responsible for all that is missing—that is, what you spend."

"I'm sure I'll be worthy of your confidence," said Miss Trowbridge.

"Be sure that you are," said Mrs. Edgeworth. "Be further advised that dear Horatio knows *nothing* about this money box. What is more, he is not to know. His nature is too refined to be troubled by such things. Please keep this information to yourself."

"Yes, madam," agreed Miss Trowbridge.

Harry, who had heard it all, was outraged. That his enemy should know of such a thing when he did not was yet another insult!

As silently as he had come, but with an indignation even greater than had existed before, Harry left his listening post.

One thing was resolved: Whatever he did would certainly include the money box.

CHAPTER 3

OUR STORY BECOMES COMPLICATED BY THE
INTRODUCTION OF THAT GREAT MAN, CONSTA-
BLE SEYMOUR NARBUT, AND HIS SECRET PAS-
SION · ALSO, A PROPOSAL AND AN UNUSUAL
ANSWER

The very same morning that Harry was plotting
against Annie Trowbridge, the town of Fairington's constable, Mr. Seymour Narbut, was stroll-
ing down the road that went by the Edgeworths'
home.

If you had asked Constable Narbut what he was
doing walking down that road that morning, he
would have informed you that he was only going
about his duty, protecting citizens. In truth, he
was there because he had fallen in love with Miss
Trowbridge.

Constable Narbut was a short, squat, square
man. A few strings of gray hair were all that
remained on his head, hardly sufficient to patch a
sock. His face was round and puffy, with three
pendulous chins. His coat was too large and made
his arms look too small. His boots pointed in
different directions as he stalked. No matter; Mr.
Narbut thought himself the fury of Fairington.

As for Miss Trowbridge, she had no idea that the constable had fallen in love with her. He had admired her from afar. He had thought of her from afar. He had, so to speak, conversed with her from afar. He had even made up his, and her, mind from afar. Indeed, it was only that morning when he had seen her walk out of town, bright and merry, that he had made up his mind to marry her.

Though Mr. Narbut was absolutely certain that Miss Trowbridge would not refuse such an important, handsome man as he, he did think it only right and proper to ask for her hand in private. Only then would he seek permission from Dr. Williams, as was the lawful thing to do.

So Mr. Narbut followed Miss Trowbridge out of town in order to propose. But when he saw her moving at a rate too brisk for his dignity—not to mention his ability—he sat himself upon a rock, the better to plan his happy future until she came back.

When at last he saw her appear along the road, some hours later, her visit to the Edgeworths over, Mr. Narbut stood up and watched her. Her long yellow skirt bobbed like an upside-down daffodil, the close bonnet shielded her from the eastern sun, and she sang with all the ease of a young girl at her freedom.

Mr. Narbut put on his gravest official face, sucked in his belly (or tried to) and with a final (but *most* important) burnish of his constable's badge, waited with impatience. Miss Trowbridge, unaware of the great moment looming before her, approached.

"Morning!" called Mr. Narbut as she drew nigh.

"Morning!" returned Miss Trowbridge cheerfully as she passed by.

"Miss Trowbridge," called Mr. Narbut, unable to hold back longer.

Annie Trowbridge stopped and turned.

"Miss Trowbridge," the constable began, "no doubt you have heard a great deal commending my character, my reputation, my general sagacity. I have noticed you from time to time, and after much wise thought—which is proof enough of my wisdom—which is to say, I'm offering you—which would be the envy of most girls —that is, would you accept—and how could you not—my proposal—which, as I said—has all been carefully considered of—you *are* a lucky girl—of marriage!"

Though Miss Trowbridge had tried very hard to follow this extraordinary speech, it took some moments for her to understand that the constable was asking her to marry him.

When she did understand, she laughed.

Mr. Narbut, expecting a very different response, was startled. "Perhaps you misunderstood," said he, his entire head blossoming into a brilliant red. "I'm offering to marry you!"

This only made Miss Trowbridge giggle some more.

"Thank you," she managed to say. But to keep herself from collapsing into outright laughter, she gathered up her skirts and ran down the road toward Fairington.

Constable Seymour Narbut was at first too astonished to understand that he had been rejected, refused, turned down. When at last he did, his only response was to shout, "Fool!" The young lady, however, was gone. Only *he* heard the word, and Mr. Narbut was not prepared to listen to anyone, no, not even to himself.

Savagely, he turned his back on Miss Trowbridge. As he walked, he counted the many follies he *now* knew were the principal points of that foolish girl, that unwanted orphan, that homely, unspeakable creature. Indeed, by the time he had finished his retreat, Miss Trowbridge had become a person only this side of being an actual criminal and liable to immediate arrest!

CHAPTER 4

YET ANOTHER SECRET! CONCERNING THE
LOVES OF MISS TROWBRIDGE · THE RESULT
THEREOF

While it was certainly true that Miss Trowbridge had no love for Constable Narbut, it did not mean that she was incapable of that tender emotion. Indeed, as she proceeded toward her own home, Mr. Narbut's talk of marriage led her mind elsewhere.

Miss Trowbridge was thinking, mostly, about the responsibility the Edgeworths had given her. She was understandably proud of the trust they were placing in her. While not the wealthiest of families, they had a reputation for being the most correct. And in such places as Fairington, if one must choose between coin and correctness, for heaven's sake, choose correctness!

The responsibility for the house and the information about the money box pleased her. But that was not the main thing: The main thing was the boy.

To Miss Trowbridge, Horatio seemed an angel, so delicate he was liable to break like a china cup. So, if nothing wrong happened, it would be very fine for her. For example, it would show her guardian, Dr. Williams, how old, how mature, and how truly adult she was.

Would she, she asked herself, be able to manage *alone?*

If she had asked me, I would have said, "Yes, of course!"

But it was herself she asked, and the more she asked, the more inclined she was to send a message to a particular person and suggest that he should come and help her. Since the Edgeworths' home was so far from town, who, she asked herself, could possibly notice such a visit?

No one. And Horatio, she thought, would hardly care.

After all, Miss Trowbridge told herself (more than once) she was *only* going to write to Mr. Nicholas Pym, *only* going to invite him to visit, *only* that she might better protect the boy. Yes, protecting Horatio was the *only* reason.

Now, it so happened that Miss Trowbridge was married to Mr. Nicholas Pym. What! Married! Why didn't I say so before? Well, you see, it was a secret. That is to say Miss Trowbridge—who I told you was not yet sixteen—had married Mr. Pym without telling her guardian for fear he might refuse permission. When she became sixteen—in just a few weeks—she would tell him.

As soon as Miss Trowbridge reached home she wrote to Mr. Pym. And as she left the letter at the post office she could not help but think how proud her guardian would be if *only* he knew how wise she was acting.

Need I inform you that she did *not* tell him?

CHAPTER 5

CONSTABLE NARBUT ACTS IN A HIGHLY PRO-
FESSIONAL MANNER AND THUS SETS AN EXALT-
ED STANDARD FOR ALL ELECTED OFFICIALS

The next day, Constable Narbut, still brooding over the great insult he had suffered at the hand and heart of Miss Trowbridge, was sitting in his office at the Fairington jail, staring moodily out from behind the barred windows at people as they passed. So it was that he observed Mr. Edgeworth emerge from the bank and head directly for the jail.

"How do you do!" Mr. Edgeworth announced as he came through the door. "My wife and I are to be in New Brunswick for a fortnight."

"You and your family will have a fine time, I'm sure," said Mr. Narbut sourly, not the least bit interested.

"Our boy is staying home," explained Mr. Edgeworth.

"Oh yes," said Mr. Narbut, vaguely recalling Harry. "Your boy. Your small boy."

"We daren't expose him to fatigue," continued Mr. Edgeworth piously. "Miss Annie Trowbridge, the minister's ward, will be minding him at home."

Once again Mr. Narbut turned scarlet. Not red. Not crimson. *Scarlet!* Somehow he felt himself again insulted. Somehow he just could not let it pass. Somehow his very sense of professional pride was pinked. Somehow—the vision leaped clearly before his eyes—somehow he just had to protect that dear, small, helpless boy from that hateful, all but criminal woman!

He swung about and leaned toward Mr. Edgeworth with the clear earnestness and cool bearing that came from disinterested professional duty. "Mr. Edgeworth," he said, "while you are gone, I shall consider it my duty to make sure nothing goes amiss!"

"Much obliged," said Mr. Edgeworth, for it was a principal point with him that his boy could not be protected enough. "But mind, Horatio is delicate by nature, fragile by inclination. Don't jostle or alarm him. If you look over things —and I'm delighted you will—be cautious!"

"Nothing to worry about there," Mr. Narbut assured him. "I'm a silent mover."

Mr. Edgeworth then handed the constable a card that bore the address where he intended to be while away. "If anything should happen, write to me at once."

"Have no fear," urged Mr. Narbut. "I've an eye for trouble before it comes. Crush it before it blooms is my motto. Do you recall Mr. Nicholas Pym, for instance?"

"Can't say that I do," said Mr. Edgeworth, who, having no interest beyond his own concerns, was already by the door.

"A good-for-nothing up to no good," Narbut informed him. "Fortunately, before he could do any real mischief, I ran him out of town and warned him not to come back. And he won't. Yes, protecting the people of this town is my job," he proclaimed. "So don't fret about a thing. Your boy will be protected."

"We thank you," returned Mr. Edgeworth, highly gratified that an elected official should show such professional interest in his own dear boy.

CHAPTER 6

GREAT DEPARTURES

The following afternoon, outside the Fairington Inn, Mr. Edgeworth's voice was heard loudly to proclaim: "The time to depart is here!"

The Edgeworths were saying goodbye, and they were late doing so. The driver of the waiting coach was looking down from his perch and muttering. A passenger who had come to Fairington with the coach was poking his head out to see what was taking so long. Of course, Mr. Narbut was there, leaning against the wall of the inn and keeping *his* eye on Miss Trowbridge. She was standing a few paces from the Edgeworths, eyes cast down in a perfect display of maiden modesty. Even her guardian, Dr. Williams, was there, making sure, from a safe distance, that all was good. In the very middle of this cocoon of protective concern stood Harry himself.

"We'll be back in ten or fifteen days, my dear," said Mrs. Edgeworth, patting and petting Harry as if he were a stuffed doll in need of reshaping.

"Miss Trowbridge shall keep house," Mr. Edgeworth reminded him. "You don't have to worry about a thing." He took the boy's hand and began to pump it as if Harry were a waterspout.

Harry, silent as usual, just stood there, all too aware that the coach driver was waiting, that Miss Trowbridge was waiting, that the passenger was waiting, that even the constable and the minister were waiting. He had wanted to go with his parents—he truly had—but now his only desire was for them to go and go quickly.

"Everything has been arranged to make you happy," said Mr. Edgeworth. "Nothing, nothing to worry about at all."

"We'll write at least three times before we get back," Mrs. Edgeworth announced. "The first letters we shall ever have written you!" And she gave him one last, crushing embrace.

Mr. Edgeworth led his wife to the coach and helped her in. Then he followed, slammed the door shut, and leaned out. "No tears, Horatio!" he cried.

The impatient driver hardly waited for the door to shut before he flung out his whip over the horses' heads with a staggering crack. Off they flew, leaving Harry, hands in pockets, cap pulled low, watching the coach disappear down the road. He was thinking: I thought they would never go.

But Miss Trowbridge, looking at Harry, con-

"No tears, Horatio!" he cried.

vinced herself that the boy's prolonged gaze meant but one thing: Helpless Harry wanted to cry, and but for his father's final words, would have done so.

While this, as you know, was nothing at all like the truth, Miss Trowbridge thought it to be, and thinking it, her heart softened further. How much, she thought, he needs protection. How glad she was that she would provide it!

When Harry could no longer see the coach, he turned about. In so doing, he discovered Miss Trowbridge looking at him closely, looking at him the way everybody always did, with a simpering, suffocating sympathy he loathed from the bottom of his heart.

"Time to go home, young master," said Miss Trowbridge sweetly, earnestly.

Master! Harry well knew that he didn't look like any master. Nor, he also knew, would she treat him remotely like one. She—the jail keeper—was only making fun.

Reluctantly, Harry crawled to the back of the wagon and stared out as they started to move. But right then he swore himself the most sacred of vows: He would show *her* who was master, and soon.

CHAPTER 7

Mr. and Mrs. Edgeworth settled into the coach for a long ride. "Only three of us," announced Mr. Edgeworth, which proved that, at any rate, he could count.

The other passenger—he had arrived with the coach from Philadelphia—was dressed like Mr. Edgeworth, though not nearly so fine.

His face, however, truly set him off as a singular person. It was positively pink, with no mustache but with a fiery fringe of bright red whiskers, which gave him the appearance of one of those old pictures of the sun, sparking rays of warm light and kindness in all directions. Red hair atop his head completed the circle, all of which seemed to give him a halo, a ring of heavenly warmth and affection.

To Mr. Edgeworth's observation this man smiled a bright, blue-eyed smile that advertised him as a kindly, friendly soul.

"Our apologies for keeping you waiting," said Mr. Edgeworth, coming instantly and favorably under the spell of the man's warmth. "Parents never do like to say goodbye to their dear children."

"We're ever so fond of him," said Mrs. Edgeworth, "and we've never left him alone this way."

"Going far?" asked Mr. Edgeworth of the man.

"I'm not exactly sure," the man replied. To hear him speak was like listening to buttermilk pour on honey.

"How can that be?" asked Mr. Edgeworth, always astonished to hear an unexpected answer.

"Oh," answered the man, not putting down his beaming smile for a jot, "I know the *what*. I just don't know the *where*. My calling takes me everywhere. And yourself," he inquired. "Are you going far?"

"New Brunswick for a fortnight," answered Mr. Edgeworth.

"On business?" asked the man.

"Oh, no," said Mr. Edgeworth, more than happy to explain. "I'm a man of independent means."

"I should have guessed," said the man. Then a troubled look crossed his sunlike face. "Your boy," he said, clearly worried, "seems rather young to be left alone."

"He *is* young," agreed Mrs. Edgeworth with a

tender tremble to her tone and a tear in her eye.

"Miss Trowbridge is there to care for him," Mr. Edgeworth reminded her, equally moved.

"Miss Trowbridge?" inquired the man, who seemed to take a great interest in small facts.

"Annie Trowbridge," explained Mrs. Edgeworth. "She's only fifteen, but—" Suddenly she turned to her husband. "Mr. Edgeworth," she exclaimed, "did you do a final reckoning with the money box?"

"All taken care of," said Mr. Edgeworth, patting her hand.

This exchange seemed to bring a particular glow of interest to the stranger's eyes. "You and your wife are very trusting," he said, "to leave a money box too."

Mr. Edgeworth, wishing to divert the subject matter under discussion, held out his hand. "My name," he said, "is Abraham Edgeworth."

The passenger returned in kind. "Mr. Jeremiah Skatch at your service. From the city of brotherly love, Philadelphia."

"And your business?" asked Mr. Edgeworth.

"A colporteur, sir. A seller of religious books to the young," he explained when he saw the blank look upon the Edgeworths' faces. "A bringer of truth, love, and bliss." So saying, he pulled from beneath his seat a large, battered traveling bag.

Opening it, he revealed stacks of little paper-covered books. "There," he said, "is *Cecil, or, The Boy Who Did Not Like His Chores.* Here, *The Little Voice Within.* Both tracts are published by the Children's Protective Society," he said, his voice reverential. "All are designed to touch the tender hearts of boys and girls, bringing them near to a more natural state of perfection."

Mrs. Edgeworth sighed.

Mr. Edgeworth asked how much they cost.

"I'm forced to charge one half-dime apiece," said the colporteur, sorrow oozing through his voice.

"Horatio must have them," cried Mr. Edgeworth, and handing over the coins he received the little books.

In just such an agreeable fashion did they talk. Mr. Skatch asked numerous questions while the Edgeworths provided the answers, all about themselves, their boy, their home. Indeed, they told the colporteur everything the man wanted to know—which was a great deal—from their politics to news about their lame cow, Lucy.

Ten miles down the road they reached the place where the horses were changed. No sooner did they stop than Mr. Skatch swung open the door and held out his hand.

"I'm happy to have made your acquaintance,"

he said. "It is always exciting to meet truly trusting people. A fair journey to you. My business calls me here. May you find in your son all that you deserve when you return."

So saying, he left, lugging his bag of tracts.

When the change of horses had been made, the coach driver peered into the compartment.

"Where's the other fellow?" he demanded.

"Got off," Mr. Edgeworth said. "His business is here."

"He paid passage to New York," insisted the driver.

"Why, I never," exclaimed Mr. Edgeworth. "Mr. Skatch is not a man who lies!"

"Let it be," returned the driver. "We're late as it is." And climbing back to his seat, off they went.

When the coach that bore the Edgeworths rolled away, out from behind a tree where he had posted himself stepped Mr. Jeremiah Skatch.

"There!" he said to himself. "A good little boy. A boy in need of protection. Left in care of a young girl. *And with a money box!*" Mr. Skatch shook his head at the wonderful ways of the world.

Gathering up his bag, Mr. Skatch then began to walk hastily *back* toward Fairington. As he walked he sang:

"The praises of my tongue
I offer to the Lord
That I was taught and learnt so young
To read His holy word!"

Even as these hopeful words poured forth from his heart, the very brilliance of the sun glowed about the face of Mr. Skatch. He knew how *he* would protect Harry.

And there you are: If ever a dear boy was in *need* of protection, if ever a dear boy was *going* to be protected, no one was going to be better protected than Helpless Harry.

CHAPTER 8

IN WHICH A STRANGE MAN APPEARS · WHAT HE DID. WHAT MISS TROWBRIDGE DID · MOST OF ALL, WHAT HARRY DID

As Miss Trowbridge drove toward the Edge-worths' home, Harry, with his cap pulled low over his face in a mood of smoldering resentment, kept himself alone at the far back of the wagon, contemplating revenge. Without having the smallest idea what he would do, he knew that he wanted to strike.

They moved down the main road for about two and a half miles, after which they turned off onto yet another road. This avenue—the Edgeworths called it that—was no more than the well-beaten wide path that led to the Edgeworth home, cutting through a thick wood that stood about the little estate like a protective moat.

Halfway through this wood, the horse came to an abrupt stop which sent the boy sprawling. With just as much speed, he sprang up and looked before them to see standing, not ten yards down the road, a man he had never seen before.

He was a tall, thin, reedy sort of fellow with a brown beard that reached his belt. His full head of hair reached his shoulders, blending with the beard, together framing a narrow face with wide eyes and long nose, a nose tending toward the red. Large hands and feet gave him the look of an ungraceful puppy. He was standing there with a rather doubtful expression on his face, while his hat fluttered against one leg like a pattering heart.

When Miss Trowbridge saw this man, she dropped the reins and clasped her hands before her breast. Harry became seriously alarmed.

"Master Horatio," said Miss Trowbridge softly, for she seemed to find it difficult to speak, "take the wagon and go on ahead. I'll be along shortly."

If those words surprised the boy—and they did—it was nothing to what the next moment brought. For Miss Trowbridge got down from the wagon and stood on the ground.

"Who is he?" Harry demanded in a nervous whisper.

"Do as I tell you," Miss Trowbridge answered, her face pinker, brighter, bolder.

Harry was uncertain what to do. Already angered by Miss Trowbridge, her behavior was now both alarming and infuriating.

"Do as I tell you!" ordered Miss Trowbridge sharply when Harry did not move.

Harry, used to taking orders, put down his feelings and questions and complied. "Yes, ma'am," he said. Taking up the reins, he gave them a shake. The horse jerked the wagon forward. Once, twice, Harry looked back, but Miss Trowbridge paid him scant heed.

Despite his castdown eyes, Harry was enormously excited and kept the wagon going as slowly as he dared, trying to steal looks at the stranger as he passed by. Not that the man noticed him; his eyes were only for Miss Trowbridge.

But Harry did not go down the road for more

than fifty yards before he pulled the horse to a sharp stop. There he leaped off the wagon, jumped into the bushes, and dashed through the woods. He was going around in a great circle right back to the very place where he had left the couple, intent as he was upon spying on them to see what they might do or say.

Harry, not wishing to be discovered, went very cautiously. There was hardly any need; the couple would not have noticed. That was clear enough when Harry saw them again. Miss Trowbridge was by the man. No! I'm being too shy! Her arms were about him, as his were about her. Then, as if that were not scandal enough to place before Harry's eyes, he saw—to his utter stupefaction —them kiss one another.

Never before had Harry seen such a thing. To the degree that he had heard of such an act he knew it only as evil. Horrified, he backed up, turned about, and racing as though the Devil himself had mangled his soul, tore back to the wagon. Into it he climbed, called to the horse, and galloped toward home.

. . . he saw—to his utter stupefaction—them kiss one another.

CHAPTER 9

A CHAPTER IN WHICH HARRY TAKES THE
BOLDEST ACTION · THE MONEY BOX TAKES ON
A VITAL ROLE IN OUR PLOT

Harry was shocked. He was amazed. He was fascinated. He was outraged. He was angry. He was indignant. But as Harry drew closer to home, all those emotions blended like so many rays of sunlight coming through a magnifying glass and focused on one point—*anger*. With the fuel of his great desire to strike at Miss Trowbridge, it is hardly to be wondered that all this concentrated energy burst into flame.

Nothing I have seen in all the world moves so quickly, so firmly, as a young person making up a mind, holding to that decision and not letting go. The snapping turtle, justly renowned for its desperate clamp of jaws, is no more than a mere pinch compared to a young person's grip upon a heartfelt decision.

Upon what, then, did Harry fasten? He caught hold of the handiest notion: *the money box*. He would take the box and hide it, and its disappearance would be blamed on Miss Trowbridge. Was there any better way for Harry to show her that he was not to be diddled?

When he reached the main gate, Harry abandoned the wagon in a leap, jumped the fence, and hurled himself toward the house. In through the door he burst. Pausing for a second, he flew up the steps and into his parents' room.

Throwing his cap to the floor, Harry dove under the bed. A quick, close examination revealed that one length of floor board was cut a tiny bit short. He pressed his fingers along its edge, pressed till they hurt, and eased the board up. It came slowly at first, but as Harry gained purchase it popped out, leaving a three-foot-long hole beneath. In the hole was the money box, no more than nine inches long and four inches wide and deep; not, I daresay, much bigger than this book. Made of wood, it had a metal strap about it for strength. A small lock kept it closed.

Slipping his hand underneath this box, Harry took it up and squirmed out from beneath the bed. Then he remembered he'd forgotten to put the board back over the hole. Back he went and fixed it. Once the box was safely tucked under an arm, he tried to decide where to hide it. But he couldn't. No, not for anything could he decide!

He looked out the window. Miss Trowbridge

and the man were just coming out of the woods. Walking casually, arm in arm, talking; once, twice, they stopped, looked at one another with a tender regard, then continued on.

Harry, shaking with nervousness, ran into the hallway, the box under his arm, in search of a hiding place. Into his own room he went. It was smaller than his parents' and had little more in it than a bed, chest, and small table. On the table was the new book, *A Kiss for a Blow*.

Harry searched around for someplace, anyplace, to put the box. He discovered nothing. Worse, a hasty look out the window showed that the couple had reached the front gate and the man was gathering in horse and wagon.

Into the guest room, which was opposite his own, Harry dashed. Again nothing.

From there he tore back to his parents' room and stood, quite close to panic. Mercifully it was then that his glance fell upon the fireplace.

Going over to it, he pushed through the morning's ashes, thinking to bury the box, but there were not ashes enough.

Stooping low, he poked his head into the fireplace and looked up. It was a big chimney, joined on one side by the downstairs flue. The main flue, into which he was looking, went straight up, straight enough so that he could see the sky. He could see that the stonework inside the chimney was rough and full of gaps. *There* was a hiding place; he would hide the box up the chimney.

Quickly, he placed the box on the floor. Shoving the ashes off to one side, he picked up the box, and stepped into the hearth where his head rose right up inside.

Still holding the box, he reached up with a free hand, took hold of one of the projecting stones, and with all his strength began to pull. A small lift, it was nonetheless a start. By pushing back against the opposite wall, as well as by kicking against a third wall, Harry managed to wedge himself yet higher.

With his back pressed as hard as he could against one wall, he let go with one hand. Blessedly he did not slip. Assured, he reached up again, took yet another grip, and pulled, all the while walking up with his feet. Again he rose. Indeed, after a few more such maneuvers he was completely within the chimney.

The light from above was bright enough for him to see the stones. They were rough, sharp, covered with ash, grime, and soot. All the same, he spied a likely crevice and reached for it, only to have the stone pop right out and come thumping down horribly on his head.

He all but fell. Only the pressure of his back against the wall kept him where he was. Undaunted, he cleared his head with a vigorous shake and looked up again. As it turned out it was not all a calamity, for the fallen stone had left a hole that looked like a perfect niche for the box. Laboriously, Harry edged his way up to it.

Still pressing with his feet and his back, Harry let go with one hand, took up the box, lifted it over his head with both hands, and swinging it forward with a mighty effort, jammed that box—*plump*—right into the hole. What's more, it stuck.

But oh, how Harry's head, back, and arms ached. He was so tired he all but dropped. Withall, he made himself come down carefully, bit by bit. When he did get down, you can imagine his horror at discovering that soot was everywhere—on him, about the hearth, all over the room. Even his feet were leaving great black footprints.

He hastened to the window. Miss Trowbridge and the man were closer yet. For a moment, Harry, fascinated, watched them.

Then he looked at his hands. Filthy. He looked at his arms. Catastrophe. He looked at himself. Calamity. With one pull he ripped off his shirt; backing up, he moved out of the room, trying to swab the floor of all the dirt festooned about. Then he recalled the stone that had fallen and struck him. Back he went to collect that, only to retreat once more, trying desperately to clean the mess as he went.

Quickly enough he saw that he was only making things worse. Frantically he pulled off his boots and scrambled to his room. There he tore off the remains of his other clothing, rolling his things into a ball; using the fallen stone as a core, he stuffed it all under his own bed.

Out from his trunk he pulled clean clothes and leaped into them, putting on stockings and shoes in a brilliant succession of hops, skips, and jumps as he went down the hall and steps.

Into the kitchen he stumbled. At the washing-up bucket he lavished water on hands, face, and arms, leaving great clumps of filth on the otherwise perfectly clean drying cloth. But even as he was drying himself he heard the front-door latch. A final leap into the main room, and he stood there, panting, as Miss Trowbridge came in. Right behind her was the stranger.

CHAPTER 10

CONCERNING MR. JEREMIAH SKATCH AND
MINISTER WILLIAMS · ALSO, SOMETHING MORE
ABOUT THE CHILDREN'S PROTECTIVE SOCIETY

Mr. Jeremiah Skatch covered ten miles in two
hours. Walking with great energy, he reached
Fairington's tall-spired church by five o'clock that
afternoon. There, a tablet by the door informed
him that the minister was the Reverend Dr.
Williams. Mr. Skatch took off his hat and
knocked cautiously on the door.

"Yes?" called out a voice from within.

Humbly, Mr. Skatch entered a small office. It
was piled with books, papers, letters, and pens, in
the midst of which was a long table covered with
more of the same. Behind this table sat Dr.
Williams himself, white-haired, white-faced,
white-handed, bending over white paper, writing, to be sure, words of white.

"Doctor Williams?" whispered Mr. Skatch.

The minister looked up. " 'Tis I," said he in a
voice no bigger than his smallest word.

"Begging your pardon," ventured Mr. Skatch,
shutting the door softly behind him, "I am
Jeremiah Skatch, purveyor of moral instruction

for the young on behalf of the Children's Protective Society."

Dr. Williams, sensing a kindred soul by the soft fluff of Mr. Skatch's words, quietly put down his pen and stood. The two shook hands. "A pleasure to meet you, Mister Skatch," he said, only a hint above a whisper. "Be seated, please."

Mr. Skatch took the edge of the chair and began: "I see, sir, that you are a scholar."

Since the minister was not at all used to being appreciated, or for that matter even noticed, it is easy to understand why he warmed to Mr. Skatch. "I try. Mr. Skatch, I do try," he said, world-weary.

"I see a man," insisted Mr. Skatch, "who labors with skill, purpose, and dedication."

In spite of himself, Dr. Williams smiled, revealing that the only whiteness he lacked, in an otherwise spotless uniform, was teeth.

"And," continued Mr. Skatch, seeing that he was touching his mark, "when I see *that,* I say to myself, why, if the pastor so labors, there are fertile fields at hand for the cultivation of *proper* youthful sentiments."

"Ah, the youth," murmured the minister with a shake of his head to acknowledge the eternal failings of the young.

"It is my honor," continued Mr. Skatch, "my

privilege, my calling, my mission in life, to bring proper reading materials to young Americans."

"A worthy, worthy task," enthused Dr. Williams, fluttering his hands together.

Pleased by his reception, Mr. Skatch brought forth some of his little books and laid them before the minister, curiously like a gambler laying out his cards. "Here's *The Lottery,* suggesting the dreadful dangers of such games. Here's Miss More's *The Shepherd of Salisbury Plain,* surely the finest piece of composition ever compiled for the edification of juveniles. Here's Lady Southdown's *The Washerwoman of Finchly Common.* Here's *The Good Boy.* Here's *The Good Girl.* Here, sir, is *Theft, A Great Sin.*

"Children are so helpless," said Mr. Skatch with new radiance in his face, "so unaware, so innocent, so in *need* of help, that I have taken it as my mission to protect them from this evil world. These books are helpful to that end. Of course," he hastened to say with humility, "it is my custom to go to the spiritual protector of the community and seek his permission to mingle amongst his flock."

"Surely," cried Dr. Williams with indignation, "none would deny you!"

"Then I have your blessing?" asked Mr. Skatch.

"My good sir, of course!"

"Naturally," Mr. Skatch confessed with humble contriteness, "I must *sell* these little moral tales. None more than a half-dime, by which, believe me, I gain no more than will carry me forward toward the fulfillment of my mission."

"Only to be expected, my good man," said Dr. Williams with much sympathy. "But how can I be of help to you?"

"If," Mr. Skatch ventured, "you could find a spare moment to write a brief introductory note suggesting, no, *hinting,* the positive benefits of my little tracts . . ."

"I shall do so at once!" insisted the minister. And putting pen to paper he wrote:

Dear Friends:

This will introduce to you Mr. Jeremiah Skatch, who represents the Children's Protective Society. He and his little moral tales are highly recommended, indeed, *urged* by me upon your worthy, if often needful, infants.

Yours faithfully,

Dr. W. W. Williams

"There!" said the minister, handing Mr. Skatch the folded letter. "May it be helpful."

"It will save many a mile, sir," Mr. Skatch assured him, "and many a soul. But," the colporteur added, "if you could provide me with the names of your congregation . . ."

Generous Dr. Williams! He wrote out the names, proclaiming them as if he were entering their names upon an honor role. Mr. Skatch listened silently until the minister said, "The Edgeworths."

"Perhaps," Mr. Skatch sliced in, "you could tell me about *them!*"

"Well you should ask," said Dr. Williams enthusiastically. "The very model of a family. Belonging to our more prosperous class. Mrs. Edgeworth is a saint. The husband profound. Their boy—"

"What about the boy?" inquired Mr. Skatch, leaning a little forward in his seat.

"An angel!" cried Dr. Williams. "Attentive. Docile. Dutiful. Timid. Always does what he's asked. Never speaks unless spoken to. Never does anything wrong. Is there anything more one can ask of a child?"

"Where can I find them?" asked Mr. Skatch.

Dr. Williams was only too willing to help the colporteur, giving him directions to the Edgeworths' home. "But alas," he warned, "the parents are gone away on a trip, although my ward, Annie Trowbridge, is caring for the boy."

"*Your* ward?" asked Mr. Skatch, who for the

first time during the interview was genuinely surprised.

"Indeed she is. You may be sure, Mr. Skatch, I would not let her venture anywhere. While I have faith in her, she is after all only a girl. She needs my protection."

Upon the steps of the church, Mr. Skatch hesitated, thinking over what the minister had told him. But having made up his mind, this man of great purpose recalled both his mission and the directions and continued on.

CHAPTER 11

CONCERNING HARRY'S REMARKABLE POWERS OF SPEECH · ALSO, INCLUDES A SURPRISING STATEMENT ABOUT THE STRANGER, WHICH YOU MAY OR MAY NOT BELIEVE

When Miss Trowbridge came into the room where Harry stood breathlessly waiting, she was positively bright. Her eyes were bright. Her cheeks were bright. Her very heart was bright.

Harry was standing perfectly still, hands tightly clasped. On his face was a look of

disapproval as could not have been missed in a
darkened room at midnight. Despite herself,
when Miss Trowbridge saw this look, she turned
pale and cast down her eyes.

Harry, resolved to say nothing, merely observed.

"I've met someone," Miss Trowbridge announced haltingly before the accusing glare of
Harry's eyes. "His name is—" But here she
stumbled and could not say what she wanted to
say, which was the truth. What had seemed
simple in thought proved impossible before the
boy. So instead she said, "This man's name is
Mister Smith. John Smith. And—and he's my
brother."

Harry looked up, taken aback by the notion
that the man might be Miss Trowbridge's
brother. He studied her face hard, and seeing that
she could not meet his eyes, he very quickly
decided that she was lying to him.

Turning, Harry looked beyond her at the man,
who had not yet entered the room. "Mr. Smith"
had not the slightest resemblance to Miss Trowbridge.

Miss Trowbridge, frightened by Harry's accusing eyes, dared not retreat. Instead she pressed
forward. "What I mean to say," she corrected
herself, "is that he's my half-brother. I haven't

seen him for twenty years. He's come unexpectedly from the West."

Harry, standing silently, only stared at the two.

"Texas," suggested Miss Trowbridge.

To her great frustration, Harry just stood there.

"I haven't seen him for a very long time," she tried.

Still Harry said nothing.

"I'm sure," she said, trying to get around Harry's silence, "that if your mother and father were here, they would make him welcome."

So saying, and as if she would set the proper example, she stepped aside and with a small motion of her hand called "Mr. Smith" into the room.

Harry looked at him hard. As for Mr. Smith —for we shall have to call him so until we learn otherwise—his eyes swept everywhere: walls, floor, anyplace they could have looked before they dared so much as glance at Harry.

Harry, assuming that what he had been told was nothing but lies, remained mute. In his mind he had already decided that it would not be enough to deal with Miss Trowbridge. No. He would have to deal with the man too.

"Young master," said the man in a voice both slow and high-pitched, "it was kind of you to invite me in."

Harry favored him with a look such as he had given Miss Trowbridge, plainly signifying that it wasn't *he* who had invited him in, but *she*. Miss Trowbridge, under the silent accusation, colored.

Mr. Smith pulled his nose once or twice, stole a few looks at Miss Trowbridge, then ran his fingers, rake-like, through his beard. "I guess you didn't invite me," he admitted. "Does that mean you're about to say you don't want me here? If that's the case, I'll go." Here again he looked to the young lady for an answer, not to Harry. Miss Trowbridge, however, was not about to answer him.

So, once again, Mr. Smith was forced to turn back to the boy, who had yet to utter a word. But all the poor man could think to do was run his fingers through his long beard and pull his nose. Finally he said, "I haven't seen her for a long time. That's reason enough to stay, don't you think?"

Harry said nothing.

"And your parents," said Mr. Smith with the breathy tone of a man driven to constant talk, "where are they?"

Harry kept his tongue.

Mr. Smith nodded in answer to his own question. "Gone, are they?" he said, with a vague hint that he had not known.

Miss Trowbridge suddenly decided to do something. "I had best prepare supper," she announced, pulling off her cap and shaking out her hair. Beating a hasty retreat, she bolted into the kitchen, leaving a discomforted Mr. Smith with the unmoving, unspeaking Harry.

Mr. Smith felt abandoned. Everywhere he looked he found Harry's stare on him. It made him flick his hat about. He coughed. He rubbed his neck. He pulled his nose. He made enough gestures to tell a novel in sign language. But it was of no use: Harry refused to speak.

"Well," said Mr. Smith finally, "I guess you just don't care for me, do you?"

Harry replied with silent affirmation.

"I can't see where I've done anything to make you feel that way," tried Mr. Smith. "I mean, I've come a ways to see her, and here you're saying, or seeming to say, because you *won't* say anything, that I shouldn't."

Harry remained mute.

"What's the matter?" whined Mr. Smith. "Don't you think we can be friends?"

Harry merely stared.

"Why not?" demanded the exasperated Mr. Smith.

Harry refused an answer.

"I suppose," said Mr. Smith, "you don't think I

am Miss Trowbridge's brother. Is that what you're thinking? Well then," he demanded, desperate for a word, any word, "Who am I, then?"

In plain truth, Harry had no idea, so he said nothing.

"A thief?" Mr. Smith taunted.

To be fair, Harry had not considered *that* notion before; but once said, he did consider it and thought that, yes, perhaps that was what the man was. In fact, perhaps Miss Trowbridge was a thief too! And maybe, he only naturally added, they *were* after the money box!

"Do you?" foolishly persisted Mr. Smith, *"Do you think I'm a thief!"*

Even as he spoke, Miss Trowbridge returned from the kitchen.

"He thinks I'm a thief," whined the exasperated Mr. Smith.

"He's nothing of the kind!" cried Miss Trowbridge, horrified.

Harry still had not said one word.

"Look here," Mr. Smith angled yet again. "Since you are master here," he said, completely passing by the question as to *who* he was, "I'll ask you straight. Can I or can I not stay for a day or two? I'll go after that. Don't you think your folks would say yes? My, uh, sister," he faltered, "says they are people of charity."

Harry considered this, looking from one to the other. *Thieves,* he thought. Yes, he was beginning to think that indeed they were just that.

"I'll sleep out in the barn," offered Mr. Smith without the slightest notion as to what was going on in Harry's head.

"For heaven's sake, child, say *something,*" scolded Miss Trowbridge. "If you don't say something, we'll take it that you agree to his staying."

Harry, refusing to be compromised, pressed his lips more tightly than ever.

"Good for you!" cried Mr. Smith, determined to take this refusal to talk as an acceptance of his staying. "You're a reasonable boy."

Harry, deciding that he could no longer bear to be in the same room with the two, held his head high and walked out of the room and out of the house, shutting the door behind him.

But when he got outside, he realized that he had forgotten his cap. Returning, he approached the room, only to hear Mr. Smith saying:

"I told you we should have told him something else. He suspects what we're up to, sure enough. See if he doesn't catch on."

To which Miss Trowbridge answered: "Fiddle-sticks. He hasn't the smallest notion in the world. Not that boy!"

These words convinced Harry that the two *were*

thieves. Not only were they thieves, but they *were* after the money box. How wise he had been to hide it!

Wheeling about, Harry, thoroughly shaken by this evidence, went into the yard trying to think what he was to do.

CHAPTER 12

MR. SKATCH DRAWS CLOSER

Following Dr. Williams' careful directions, it was not long before Mr. Jeremiah Skatch stood looking over the Edgeworth house. Though it was rather smaller than Mr. Edgeworth had led him to believe, Mr. Skatch bolstered himself with the thought of large gifts in small packages.

A house of two floors, its brown-gray stone gave the building strength and dignity. The second floor had but two rooms, three windows in all, which the setting sun lit up like diamonds. At the end of the slate-covered roof stood a chimney. By the kitchen-side chimney a large apple tree rose high, laden with almost-ripe fruit.

Having satisfied himself that all was as it should be, Mr. Skatch went back up the road, but not very far. Stepping off the road, he walked into the woods in search of a level place. When he found one, he removed his hat and coat and hung them on a tree. Rolling up his sleeves, he set about to work.

He gathered as many branches from the ground as he could, taking up only long ones, not resting till he had himself a handsome pile. Then he began to lay them up against yet another tree, tops together, forming a semicircle on the ground. He was making a lean-to.

Mr. Skatch worked with energy, sweating hard, collecting more branches to lay upon the ones he had already set down. When the wall was done, he crawled underneath and snapped off the dangling bits.

His shelter built, he contented himself with gathering wood pieces and bringing them inside. Pocket flint, stone, and much close work soon brought him a small, warming fire, just enough to cut the chill from the air.

From his bag Mr. Skatch pulled a piece of bread, and with his back against the tree he ate slowly, knowing the bread was—for the moment —all that he had.

When he had finished his meal, he continued sitting and thinking out the next day, just how he would proceed. Having made his decisions, he reached into his bag again and took out one of his little books, *The Duty of Children to Do Some Good in the World.* He grimaced as if he were about to taste bad but necessary medicine. Still, he read the little book through, from time to time even committing one of the passages to memory.

When Mr. Skatch was sure it was late enough so that he would not be observed, he pushed a circle of earth around his small fire so that it would not spread. Then, backing out of the lean-to, he quietly made his way toward the Edgeworth house. He did this with the greatest of care, for he had no desire to be seen. Not yet.

CHAPTER 13

HARRY'S SUSPICIONS AND WHAT CAME OF THEM

That night, Harry sat at the table alone while Miss Trowbridge, treating him as if he were master of the house, stayed in the kitchen with Mr. Smith.

Feeling miserable, Harry watched the candle burn down, listened to the crickets, gazed at the winking hearth, and thought about the box hidden in the upstairs chimney. As he poked about his food he wondered what to do now that he had discovered he was among thieves.

There was conversation in the kitchen, but the two adults kept their voices low. Harry, of course, was certain it was to keep him from overhearing.

Three times Mr. Smith laughed out loud. Each time he did so, Miss Trowbridge said, "Shhh! He'll hear you!"

Harry's anger burned.

When Miss Trowbridge cleared the dishes from Harry's table, she said, "Your parents told me I was to hear you read from your book before you went to bed."

Reluctantly, Harry went upstairs to his room and took his *Peter Parley* reader from the chest, wondering where he had left his cap. He had not been able to find it.

Coming downstairs, he found Mr. Smith sitting in his father's chair (where no one else was ever permitted to sit) smoking a pipe. The smell of tobacco, not allowed in the house, made Harry's nose itch.

Harry, saying nothing, handed the book to Miss Trowbridge, then took his regular recitation place before the fire, opposite where Mr. Smith was sitting.

Miss Trowbridge bent forward to catch the

candlelight until she found the proper page. Then she began to read the questions printed at the bottom.

"When did Columbus come to America?" she read.

"Fourteen ninety-two," replied Harry.

"What was he seeking?"

"The riches of India."

"What did he find?"

"America."

"For whom did he discover America?"

"The King and Queen of Spain."

"Who came after Columbus?"

"The Spaniards."

"What were they seeking?"

Harry stole a glance at Mr. Smith to see if the man was looking at him. He was.

"What were they seeking?" Miss Trowbridge repeated.

"Gold," said Harry, giving a hard look at Mr. Smith.

"How did they get it?" went on Miss Trowbridge.

"By taking it from the Indians by *lies*,"—a look to Miss Trowbridge—"*theft*,"—a look to Mr. Smith—"and *murder!*"—an appeal to Heaven.

Flustered, Miss Trowbridge snapped the book shut. "That's quite enough," she announced.

"You may go to bed. Say your prayers before you sleep."

Taking up his candle and book, Harry paused at the first step. "Where is Mister Smith going to sleep?" he asked.

"I don't know," replied Miss Trowbridge.

"He promised to sleep in the barn," Harry reminded her.

Miss Trowbridge looked at Mr. Smith.

"If the young master wishes to have it that way," Mr. Smith said with a tired shrug, "I'm happy to oblige."

In his room Harry kneeled against his bed and closed his eyes. Outwardly praying, he was actually only wishing he could think what to do.

He felt a touch on his shoulder. It was Miss Trowbridge; her tread had been so soft that he hadn't heard.

"What's the matter?" she asked. "Why are you acting the way you are?"

Harry, refusing to speak, only looked at her.

"Are you frightened of Mister—Smith?"

Harry shook his head.

Trying to make up her mind, she sat down on Harry's bed, thinking that she should tell the boy who the man truly was. But fearfulness made her keep her silence; she couldn't speak the truth.

"Have you said your prayers?" she asked. "A

body never knows but the Lord might take them when they sleep."

Harry, considering this nothing less than a threat of murder, merely said, "Yes."

"Goodnight then," she said, and started for the door. Even then she paused as if she really would say something. But no, she only passed out of the room.

As Miss Trowbridge went downstairs Harry listened. After a long wait he heard what he was hoping for, the sound of the front door closing. He looked out the window.

In the moonlight he saw Mr. Smith, candle in hand, walking slowly toward the barn. Halfway there he stopped and looked back. Suddenly Harry realized that Mr. Smith was looking at his window. Instantly, he pulled out of sight, then, with greater care, peeked out again.

Mr. Smith, looking like Harry's notion of the Devil, stood awhile, turned, and continued toward the barn, which he entered. Harry kept his watch, expecting the man to come out again. When he did not, Harry turned toward the door. But hardly had he taken a step in that direction when he heard a step right outside his room.

He dared not move.

CHAPTER 14

IN WHICH THE FORCES OF LAW AND ORDER
BEGIN TO EXERT THEMSELVES

It has been a while now since we last saw him, so it is quite possible that you have forgotten one of the most important characters of this history. Who, you ask, can that be? Surely, you have not forgotten the "Fury of Fairington," the "Silent Mover," the "Great Protector"—I give only *some* of his names—in short, is it possible you have forgotten Constable Seymour Narbut?

But what has he been doing all this while? Did he not swear to do his duty to protect our Harry? Let me be the first to assure you that, having so promised, he *will* do just as he said. And this is what he did:

That very evening the good constable took a large dinner at the public house. When he decided it was late enough—and there was no more food to be had—he announced loudly that he was going to bed.

In fact he did no such thing!

As far as Mr. Narbut was concerned, he could see more at night than most folks noticed by day. Wasn't it nighttime when he had picked out that good-for-nothing Nicholas Pym lurking suspiciously about the church house? It was.

Mr. Narbut took his customary turn around town, then left when he was certain he was unobserved. He took no horse—a horse would have made too much noise. Soon, he was at the end of the road, looking toward the Edgeworth home. The house stood out clearly, a candle burning behind the main-floor window. All was dark.

Then the front door opened and to Mr. Narbut's surprise a man stepped out, a man holding a candle. The constable squinted his eyes to see who it was, but he was too far away and could only tell that it was a man. Mr. Narbut tried to recall if Mr. Edgeworth had someone else staying at the house. But aside from the small boy and Miss Trowbridge, he was certain no one was supposed to be there.

Mr. Narbut watched as the man crossed in front of the house, paused, looked back, then went on toward the barn, which he entered. Inside the house the constable observed a candle moving about.

What, Mr. Narbut asked himself with mounting excitement, was happening? He kept his place, listening, watching.

As he waited, the crackling of a twig somewhere in the woods reached his ears. The first time he discounted it as the sound of an animal. But it came a second time and he knew it was not a beast.

Reminding himself that Mr. Edgeworth had expressly told him to keep out of sight, the noble constable, glad for the excuse, stepped back deeper into the shadows.

CHAPTER 15

HARRY DISCOVERS WHAT MISS TROWBRIDGE IS ABOUT · HE ALSO MEETS MR. JEREMIAH SKATCH · WHAT COMES OF ALL THIS

At the sound of the step outside his door, Harry dared not move. The door opened two inches, Miss Trowbridge appeared, then withdrew, closing the door behind her. Harry heard her pass quietly down the hall.

Hastening to the door, he opened it a crack and spied out, not at all sure where Miss Trowbridge was or what she was doing. With sudden understanding he knew: She was in his parents' room.

What could she be doing there? For Harry, the

answer came with ease: She was looking for the money box.

With eyes pushed up against the door crack Harry kept watching till light appeared at the end of the hall. Sure enough, Miss Trowbridge stepped forward, candle in hand. Over one arm she had a blanket. On top of the blanket was Harry's cap.

Seeing his cap, Harry recalled—or thought he recalled—that he had left it by his parents' bed. Or was it *under* the bed? And how could Miss Trowbridge have found it unless she herself had gone beneath the bed.

That thought led to yet another. Since Miss Trowbridge had gone under the bed to look for the box—and Harry had no doubts whatsoever about that—then she must have discovered it was gone. If she discovered that, then with equal certainty, she would tell her fellow thief what had happened.

So when Miss Trowbridge went down the stairs, Harry, fairly jumping with nervousness, silently followed. When he heard her open the front door, he dashed back to his own room to observe from the window.

Just as he had suspected, Miss Trowbridge headed directly for the barn. Though she no longer had the cap with her, she did have the blanket.

Harry made a quick decision: Down the steps he clattered, not caring what noise he made. Snatching his cap from the table, he ran through the kitchen and out of the house by the back door. As he did so, he looked toward the barn, only to see the door open. Out came Miss Trowbridge.

Harry ducked behind the apple tree.

Straight on to the house the young lady came, entering by the front door.

Suddenly Harry felt ill. By taking his cap from the table—something he was certain Miss Trowbridge would notice—he had given himself away. Now certainly she would run to Mr. Smith and raise the alarm. The mere thought of that danger caused Harry to burst from the protection of the house and, avoiding the roadway, to leap over the fence and hurl himself toward the woods, fully expecting Mr. Smith to come flying out behind him.

Reaching the woods, he burst among the trees, only to crash headlong into Mr. Jeremiah Skatch.

. . . *he burst among the trees, only to crash headlong into Mr. Jeremiah Skatch.*

CHAPTER 16

THE MEETING OF HARRY AND MR. JEREMIAH
SKATCH · WHAT CAME OF IT

The force of the collision knocked Harry to the ground, but just as quickly he was caught up and held tightly from behind by powerful hands. Harry, frantic, began to kick his legs wildly in an attempt to free himself.

"Stop it!" came a harsh command as Mr. Skatch gripped him so tightly that Harry could hardly breathe.

"Let me go!" sputtered the boy.

"Only if you don't run away," came the harsh reply. "If you do, I'll smash you down again. Understand me?"

"Yes," cried Harry weakly.

"All right then. Mind, don't fool."

Harry, finding himself released, dropped into a heap on the ground. Looking up, he saw Mr. Skatch. Mr. Skatch, who had seen him earlier in the day from the coach window, recognized him.

"Ah!" said Mr. Skatch in a remarkably sweeter tone. "It's *you,* Horatio. I'd no idea. I beg to hope I did not hurt you." And he leaped to pick up the boy and brush him off.

"Who are you?" Harry asked, rubbing his arms, which were still sore from Mr. Skatch's painful grasp.

"I'm your friend, Mister Jeremiah Skatch."

"I never heard of you before," said Harry cautiously.

"Nevertheless, my boy, I *am* your friend. But what's the matter?" asked Mr. Skatch. "What's a bold, brave boy like you running about like this?"

Pause and consider Mr. Skatch's use of the words "bold" and "brave." It is a sad but true fact—an unfortunate fact, I hasten to say—that those who wish to harm the minds of youth seem to understand them far better than those who wish to keep them pure. So painful is this fact that over the years researchers have explored the question whether or not being young is truly necessary, or, for that matter, even a good thing. There seems to be a general agreement among those who love children most, that if childhood could be avoided altogether, children would be much better off.

The point is, I am afraid that Harry was *pleased* to have those words "brave" and "bold" applied to him. It made him look upon Mr. Skatch with instant favor.

"Your father and mother," said Mr. Skatch

soothingly, "are friends of mine. They sent me here to be with you."

"Did they?" said Harry, who, despite himself, was a little comforted by the thought.

"Now of course," continued Mr. Skatch, "I know you don't need help. You're a bold, bright boy who knows his own way. But why were you crashing through the woods?"

Harry looked up at the man curiously. It certainly was pleasing to hear those things said about him. Still, he was doubtful. "Are you really a friend of my parents?" he asked.

"Of course I am," the colporteur returned. "They've gone to New Brunswick, haven't they? I wouldn't have known that if they hadn't told me, now would I? They'll come back in a fortnight. Left today by coach from Fairington. Promised to write to you. And you never have received letters from them before, have you? I know. I'm not likely to know such things without their being my friends, am I?"

"No, sir," replied Harry, impressed.

"Now, my fearless fellow," said Mr. Skatch. "Why, courageous boy that you are, were you running through the night?"

Harry considered: He was flattered by the man's words. He was also really worried about Miss

Trowbridge and her friend. So he said, "I was afraid."

"You? Afraid? I *am* surprised. Of what?"

"Miss Trowbridge."

"Ah," said Mr. Skatch tenderly. "What about her has frightened you?"

"It's not just her," explained Harry, warming to the sympathetic tone. "There's a man with her. He's a thief. They both are."

"A thief!" cried Mr. Skatch, truly alarmed.

"He's a bad one, sir," Harry continued, "with horrible eyes, a scraggly beard that makes him look wild, and an unpleasant voice. She says he's her brother, but I don't think so."

"Don't you?"

"I saw them—kissing," whispered Harry.

"Did you?" asked Mr. Skatch. "But have they done anything that makes you certain they are—*thieves?*"

Harry hesitated before speaking, a little troubled by his own thoughts. "The money box under my parents' bed," he whispered. "It's gone!"

"*Gone!*" exclaimed Mr. Skatch, truly outraged. "You mean to tell me that *they* have taken it?"

Carefully, Harry said, "It's no longer under the bed."

For a moment Mr. Skatch said nothing, but his look of anger was awful. Such indignation. Such fury. Such—what shall I say—frustration!

"Not under the bed? Have they left the house with it?" the colporteur demanded.

"Oh, no, sir, I'm sure they haven't."

"Why?" snapped the man. "Why are you sure?"

"I know where it is."

"Do you!"

Harry nodded.

"*Where?*"

Harry considered. "I don't think I should say."

"Why not?"

"Please, sir, I think it would be better if they were caught with it gone. If I were to bring it to you for safekeeping, why, no one would believe *they* took it. I know you would, but no one else. But if I showed everybody where it was, they would be punished, wouldn't they?"

Mr. Skatch looked at the boy with astonishment, but that look gradually changed to a radiant smile. "What a clever boy you are!" he said, with such clear pleasure that Harry found himself very proud indeed. "Well done! Well done indeed!" said the colporteur. "Just two questions. Do you not like Miss Trowbridge?"

"I detest her."

"And you want her to be punished for her wickedness."

"Oh yes, sir, I do!"

"You are a bright boy," said Mr. Skatch. "So I am going to ask you to do a brave thing. It would be better if you went back home. Don't worry! I, who am your friend, shall be looking on. Tomorrow morning I shall come to your house and see what I shall see. Mind, don't let them know you know me. Can you manage that? Of course you can. You're a very intelligent boy.

"Now, where is this other man, the thief, staying?" Mr. Skatch asked.

"In the barn, sir."

"I'll watch that too. Now, you had best return home. Don't worry about a thing. I'll be there early."

"Just one thing, sir."

"What's that?"

"I'd rather be called Harry."

"Harry it is!" laughed Mr. Skatch, and with a gentle shove sent the boy on his way.

Returning home without incident, Harry replaced his cap on the table and then crept upstairs to his room. There, without bothering to get out of his clothes, he tumbled into bed happier than he could remember being before.

As he drifted off to sleep his head filled with a fluff of thoughts: how he disliked Miss Trowbridge; how he thought she was a thief; how she *was* a thief; how he was glad she was a thief.

Added to those thoughts, like nuts atop a gob of ice cream, were Mr. Skatch's words: "brave, clever, strong, intelligent. . . ."

Harry actually went to sleep with a smile upon his lips!

CHAPTER 17

A CHAPTER IN WHICH CONSTABLE SEYMOUR
NARBUT TAKES DECISIVE ACTION AND THERE-
BY DOES HIS DUTY

Constable Narbut, aware that someone else was hiding in the woods beside himself, decided to wait and keep his eyes on the barn and the house, where he reckoned Annie Trowbridge was.

And so it was that he saw Miss Trowbridge go to the barn and return. But shortly after, to his great astonishment, he saw the Edgeworths' little boy run pell-mell across the field away from the house, leap into the woods, and crash.

After that came the distinct sound of voices.

Greatly troubled, but just as greatly cautious, Mr. Narbut moved through the woods toward where he thought the voices were coming from, only to lose his sense of direction when these voices lowered. Not sure where to go, he stood still.

When he did spy Harry again, he was standing and talking to someone whom Mr. Narbut did not recognize.

The noble constable of Fairington's first thought was to rush forward. His second, more compelling thought was to stay still. After all, he carefully reasoned, the boy didn't seem to be in any real danger. More important, had not Mr. Edgeworth positively told him not to make the boy aware that he was about? Mr. Narbut, a man given to following instructions, particularly when they suited his inclinations, remained where he was.

A short time thereafter Mr. Narbut saw Harry run back into the house. When the constable turned to the spot where the stranger had been, he was gone.

Mr. Narbut did consider following him into the woods, but decided that was an unwise thing to do. After all, he reminded himself, it was the boy he was protecting, and the boy was safely home.

Accordingly, Mr. Narbut turned about and hastened back to Fairington. In his room he took to his chair, folded his hands over his large belly, and began to think.

He had no idea what was going on at the Edgeworth place, but he knew it was trouble, just as he knew that Miss Trowbridge was the cause.

It called for decisive action.

Picking up pen and paper he wrote out the following:

Mr. Abraham Edgeworth, Esq.

All is NOT well at your home. Are you truly certain that Annie Trowbridge can be trusted? But, do NOT be alarmed. *I* have everything under control.

Yours faithfully,

Constable S. Narbut

Early the next morning this hard-working man took the trouble to personally hand his letter to the driver of the early stage, determined that the Edgeworths should have the letter that same day.

That done, this thoroughgoing professional returned to his room and caught up on some of the sleep he had sacrificed to duty. But then, there was no official so keen on his obligations as Constable Seymour Narbut.

CHAPTER 18

ALL IN ALL AN EVENTFUL CHAPTER: MR.
JEREMIAH SKATCH COMES FORWARD · HARRY IS
PLEASED · MISS TROWBRIDGE IS TROUBLED ·
THE MAN CALLED MR. SMITH IS SHY

Early next morning Mr. Jeremiah Skatch, gathering up his bag of tracts, passed through the woods and along the road until he could see Mr. Smith chopping wood by the barn, his back toward him.

Mr. Skatch set a smile to his face, a thing he did with great skill, and proceeded slowly down the path, loudly whistling a hymn. At the gate he paused.

"Morning!" he cried out when Mr. Smith gave not the slightest sign of noticing him.

Startled, Mr. Smith dropped his ax and spun about. "Morning," he said, after a moment's study of the smiling man in top hat, jacket, and traveling bag.

"Do I, sir, have the pleasure of speaking to Mister Edgeworth?" asked Mr. Skatch sweetly.

"Not here," answered Mr. Smith.

Mr. Skatch put on a look of surprise and disappointment. "Will he be back soon?"

"I don't know," replied Mr. Smith evasively.

"Well, then," asked Mr. Skatch briskly. "Mistress Edgeworth?"

"No, not here either."

"Are you their man?" wondered Mr. Skatch.

"Maybe, maybe not," returned Mr. Smith. "Who are you?"

Mr. Skatch accepted this question as an invitation to come forward. "My name is Jeremiah Skatch of Philadelphia, the city of brotherly love. I'm a colporteur, sir, representing the Children's Protective Society. Is there *anyone* at home?" he wondered, bringing the minister's letter from his pocket.

"I'll have to see," said Mr. Smith.

Mr. Smith went into the house, and within moments Miss Trowbridge returned, followed by Harry. The boy, recognizing Mr. Skatch as the man he had met the night before, hung back, unsure as to what was about to happen. As for Mr. Smith, being naturally cautious, he went around the house and stood by the apple tree, looking on.

When Mr. Skatch saw Miss Trowbridge, he lifted his hat in a gallant salute and smiled brilliantly.

"How do you do, ma'am. I am Mister Jeremiah Skatch, seller of books for children on behalf of the Children's Protective Society." With a bow he offered Dr. Williams' letter of introduction. Miss Trowbridge accepted it and read it.

Knowing the handwriting of her guardian, Dr. Williams, she had no reason to doubt that Mr. Skatch was anything but what he claimed.

"Mister and Mistress Edgeworth are gone," she said politely. "And they won't be back for some time."

"Gracious!" cried Mr. Skatch. "Not the start of a good day. It's even more unfortunate when I see that *there* is a young boy who might well be served by the study of such little tokens as I offer." So saying, he pulled two little books from his bag, one of which he thrust into Harry's hand, the other into Miss Trowbridge's.

"Only the *best* of literature," he assured them. "Uplifting. Moral. Properly written from the proper point of view. These books will fill the minds of American youth with nothing but right thoughts, right morals, right ideals, right *tendencies!* You, ma'am, have a copy of *Nelly Bly, The Girl Who Did Not Know Right from Wrong.* It tells the sorrowful tale of a young woman who, by *not* listening to her protectors, receives, alas, her just reward. You, young man," said Mr. Skatch to Harry, "have *The Dangers of Dining Out, or, Hints to Those Who Would Make Home Happy, to Which Is*

Added the Confessions of a Maniac. Only one half-dime apiece."

"I have no leave to buy such things," said Miss Trowbridge, truly apologetic, as she attempted to return the book Mr. Skatch had given her.

He refused. "Did not your master insist that you treat the boy well? In no wise different than he would have done himself? Perhaps if you do *not* provide him with one of these excellent moral tales, you will be neglecting your duty. Might not *you*, ma'am, be the cause of his ruination?"

Miss Trowbridge, who in the warmth of Mr. Skatch's words had turned a shade pinker, mumbled, "I don't think so."

The colporteur, a sensitive man, noticed and pressed on. "Well, I admit to this: You *seem* to be a good woman. You *appear* to be a fine soul, one whom I *presume* knows her obligations. One *assumes* you to be modest, refined, and honest. But then, my dear," he added, with a sudden flash in his eye, "being mortal, I suppose that even *you* are capable of sin!"

It was as if Mr. Skatch had touched a button marked *Secret!* Miss Trowbridge, on hearing his words, lost whatever sense of ease she had, and would not, could not, dared not, look upon him again.

Mr. Skatch, noticing this very well indeed,

. . . "being mortal, I suppose that even you *are* capable of sin!"

acted as if nothing had happened. Taking advantage of Miss Trowbridge's confusion, he went to Harry and shook his hand. "What's your name, my bucko?" he asked, not neglecting a conspiratorial wink.

"Harry, sir."

"I should like to be your friend, Harry," proclaimed Mr. Skatch. "Indeed, I *shall* be your friend. You may have that book for free. It shall bind our friendship." Taking out a stub of slate pencil from his pocket he took back the book and wrote upon the flyleaf:

> *To Hero Harry*
> *From his admirer,*
> *Jeremiah Skatch*

Handing Harry the book, Mr. Skatch drew his arm around the boy's shoulder, pulled him closer, and whispered in his ear, "You're doing fine, my friend. We'll get her yet!"

Releasing the boy, Mr. Skatch turned to Miss Trowbridge. "Very well," he said. "I wish you a good day. I'll trouble you no more, but shall return when the Edgeworths come back." So saying, he bowed and tipped his hat, then snatched the book from her hand.

Mr. Skatch gathered up his bag and started

down the path, bursting into song at the top of
his voice:

> *"Almighty God, thy piercing eye*
> > *Strikes through the shades of night*
> *And our most secret actions lie*
> > *All open to thy sight!*
>
> *There's not a sin that we commit*
> > *Nor wicked word we say*
> *But in thy dreadful book 'tis writ*
> > *Against the judgment day!"*

Harry followed Mr. Skatch with his eyes,
basking in the glow of conspiracy with the
colporteur, feeling nothing but gratification for
his friendship and protection.

Miss Trowbridge was not so happy. She was, in
fact, very upset. "What was that he said to you?"
she demanded of Harry as soon as Mr. Skatch was
out of the yard.

Harry merely drew himself up and looked
smug.

Miss Trowbridge, feeling queerly, said,
"There's your Bible to read before breakfast.
Please make ready!"

Harry, only too pleased to go, went right into
the house, shutting the door behind him with a
slam.

CHAPTER 19

CONCERNING THE CONSCIENCE OF MISS TROW-
BRIDGE · MR. SMITH GOES ON A MISSION ·
HARRY READS A BIT OF THE BIBLE · THE
SINGULAR RESULTS OF THAT · ALSO, A SURPRISE
VISITOR · IN SHORT, A VERY FULL CHAPTER
THAT YOU WON'T WANT TO MISS

Here!" said Mr. Smith as soon as Harry had
gone into the house. "Who was that man? He's
very familiar with the boy."

"I never saw him before," said Miss Trowbridge, still looking to where Mr. Skatch had
disappeared into the woods as if, just by looking,
she could solve the puzzle.

"What was that letter he showed you?"

"From Doctor Williams," explained Miss Trowbridge. Her worry, feeding on a bad conscience,
was beginning to grow. "He must be what he says
he is, but he looked at me so oddly, as if he could
read my mind. And he *hinted* too," she said,
blushing over the errors of her ways. "What name
did you give him?" she asked Mr. Smith.

"Why, do you think he knows who I am?" he
said, becoming alarmed himself.

Miss Trowbridge's agitation grew even more. "I

don't know," she admitted. "You'd better follow him and see where he goes."

Agreeing at once, Mr. Smith picked up the ax he had been using and knocked it into the cutting log. Then, ambling off, he started after Mr. Skatch.

"Be careful," Miss Trowbridge called out after him, watching till he was lost behind the trees.

When he had gone, Miss Trowbridge shook her head; a feeling of discomfort had come over her, from which she could not rid herself. With a sigh she went into the kitchen where Harry was waiting, the Bible on the table before him.

"Is your brother coming to hear me read?" he asked.

"He's got chores to do," Miss Trowbridge told him, her mind on other things. "Please get on with it."

Just by looking at her Harry could see how upset Miss Trowbridge was. That pleased him. He knew it was Mr. Skatch who had upset her, and Harry liked the man even more for that.

Wondering if he might not make her even more upset, he turned the pages of the Bible until he found the Book of Psalms. Tracing with his finger till he reached the spot he wanted, he began to read: " 'Blessed is the man that walketh not in the counsel of the ungodly, nor standeth in the way of sinners, nor sitteth in the seat of the scornful.' "

Miss Trowbridge, who had not been minding, suddenly caught the words and reacted by looking at the boy with absolute horror.

"Why are you reading *that?*" she demanded.

Harry looked up innocently. "Would you rather I didn't?"

"No," she faltered. "Of course not. Go on."

Harry skipped a few lines to get to the real testing part: " 'The ungodly are not so but are like the chaff which the wind driveth away. . . . But the way of the ungodly shall perish.' "

Harry looked up at Miss Trowbridge. The woman looked positively sick. For a moment he thought he'd gone too far. "Are you all right?" he asked.

"Yes," she said, but so weakly that it gave quite the opposite meaning to her word.

"I think I had better stop reading," said Harry, gratified to see Miss Trowbridge look and act so guilty over the words "the ungodly shall perish."

With great agitation she put dishes out only for Harry.

"Aren't you going to eat?" asked the boy.

"I'll wait for my brother," she answered faintly.

Her reply was instantly buried under a great

thumping noise from the front door, a noise so loud, so sudden, as to make both people jump. Harry, glad for an excuse to bolt, ran out of the kitchen and opened the main door. It was Constable Seymour Narbut.

"You know me, don't you, boy?" asked Mr. Narbut.

"Yes, sir," said Harry, "You're the constable."

"Smart boy. I suspect you're missing your folks."

"Yes, sir," said Harry dutifully, taking a quick look back over his shoulder to see if Miss Trowbridge had remained in the kitchen. Seeing that she had hung back, he went up to the constable and whispered, "Sir, my father's money box is missing."

"Is it!" cried Mr. Narbut. "Where's Miss Trowbridge?"

Like an actress on cue, Miss Trowbridge herself came out of the kitchen where she had been trying to gather the courage to tell Harry the whole truth of her situation and beg his forgiveness. But when she saw who had come, she stopped stiffly where she was.

"Mister and Mistress Edgeworth are away," she said icily.

"I know all about that," returned Mr. Narbut.

"It's you I need a word with. If you don't object, that is."

"Go outside, Harry," said Miss Trowbridge, annoyed that the constable had come—or so she thought—to make yet another proposal of marriage to her.

Harry had no desire to leave, but he had no choice. So out he strolled over to the apple tree where he pulled down an apple. He took one bite, but finding it hard, turned to fling it away. It was then that he saw the ax in the chopping block. Right off he guessed that Mr. Smith had fled. Putting two and two together (and making five), he decided that Mr. Narbut had frightened him away.

Pleased, Harry took up the hard apple and flung it at the ax. A fine thrower—if baseball had been invented, Harry would have been a pitcher —he hit the ax perfectly, splitting the fruit cleanly in two. In fact, while he waited for Mr. Narbut to come out he threw and split three more apples, each one a perfect strike.

CHAPTER 20

CONSTABLE NARBUT SETS FORTH HIS OBJEC-
TIONS · MISS TROWBRIDGE MAKES AN AMAZING
DISCOVERY

Constable Narbut was feeling smug. He was the
law. He was power. The young lady who had
laughed at him was standing before him. Not that
he had any intention of mentioning *that*. Not in
the least! He was there *only* to do his professional
duty of protecting the boy. So he just folded his
arms over his stomach and spoke with great
majesty.

"I don't wish to alarm the boy unduly," he
began, "but seeing as it was you who was left in
charge, Mister Edgeworth asked me to have a look
about while he was gone."

"He said nothing to me," returned Miss
Trowbridge stoutly.

"No, I suspect he wouldn't," agreed Mr.
Narbut. "Point is, I'm a silent mover, Miss
Trowbridge. I came by late last night and I
noticed a few things. One, I saw a man come out
of this house and go into the barn."

Miss Trowbridge's face went perfectly white.
Narbut noted it and felt the better for it.

"Two," he continued, "I spied that boy wandering about during the night."

"The boy?" cried Miss Trowbridge, startled again. "I thought he was asleep."

"I daresay you did," gloated Mr. Narbut, enjoying her great discomfort. "Three, that boy met someone out in the woods. I suppose," he said in a voice heavy with sarcasm, "you didn't know that either."

Miss Trowbridge was so taken aback by what Mr. Narbut had said that she could not have answered anything, no, not even if she could have given reasonable explanations about any of it.

"Finally," said Mr. Narbut, secure that she was at the point of utter defeat, "it's my understanding that Mister Edgeworth's money box is gone. My suggestion is this: I'll take the boy. You return the box. No questions asked. I'll keep everything safe and respectable till the Edgeworths return."

First Miss Trowbridge had been insulted. Then she had been startled. But when he had so much as told her that she was not to be trusted, that she was a thief, she was so angry she could not even speak.

Nonetheless, Mr. Narbut pushed on. "Mind, if anything does happen to that boy or that money box, why, don't you see, I'll be duty bound to say what I've seen. All of it."

Miss Trowbridge burst out with great indignation, "Because I laughed at you!"

Constable Seymour Narbut dismissed this absurd notion with the sneer it deserved. "Miss Trowbridge," he patiently explained, "my job is to protect that boy and Mister Edgeworth's property. It's not for me to say what *your* reputation will be, but—"

"*I've done nothing wrong!*" protested Miss Trowbridge.

"Maybe, maybe not," the constable returned. "Why don't you just admit that you're incapable of doing your duty, too young to manage, foolish, and maybe a thief as well as a few other things I could mention, but won't because I'm a gentleman. You just go on back and take care of Doctor Williams. I'll take over and tell the Edgeworths you weren't up to the job and say no more."

Miss Trowbridge proudly drew herself up. "The Edgeworths left no such instructions," she said. "I can protect the boy myself."

"I doubt it," said Mr. Narbut. "What about the money box?"

"I must ask you to leave," shouted Miss Trowbridge, her voice trembling with rage.

Mr. Narbut put on his hat and tapped it low over his brow. "Miss Trowbridge," he said, determined to have the last word, "Mister

Edgeworth is a particular friend of mine. I don't want him or his boy to come to any grief. You've only to call upon me and I'll know my duty."

So saying, he left.

No sooner did the constable shut the door than Miss Trowbridge flew to it and latched it tight. Leaning against the door, she went through all that Mr. Narbut had said.

She guessed well enough who he had seen coming out of the house. But she was even more distressed that Harry had run about at night, though clearly no harm had come to him. As to whom he had spoken, she had not the slightest idea. As for the money box, it was totally outrageous. To think that anyone would even suggest that she had stolen it!

Taking a quick look outside, she saw that the constable was talking to the boy. A sudden decision brought her up to the Edgeworths' bedroom. She would take up the money box and give it to Narbut then and there, thus proving how innocent she was.

Down beneath the bed she went. And it took but seconds for her to locate the false board. Up it came. Into the hiding place she looked. The box was *not* there.

If ever a heart failed, it was the heart of Miss Annie Trowbridge!

CHAPTER 21

THE CONSTABLE AND HARRY CONFER · WAR IS
DECLARED · A STRATEGY IS SET

Harry was lounging about by the apple tree when the constable came out. With a general swagger of achievement, Narbut strolled over to where the boy was.

"Don't you worry about a thing, boy," said Narbut, patting Harry on the head. "Everything is under my control."

"Please, sir," Harry whispered, shrugging off the pat, a thing he detested. "Can I tell you something else?"

" 'Course you can; no better person on earth to tell things to than me."

"There's a man who came here yesterday," confided Harry. "She says he's her brother. I don't think he is."

"She hasn't any brother," snapped Mr. Narbut. "What's his name?"

"She said 'Mister Smith,' " and then Harry gave the constable an accurate description of the stranger.

"By God!" thundered Mr. Narbut. "That's Nicholas Pym. I ran him out of town and told him to keep out. Where is he?"

"He left just before you came."

"He must have seen me coming and got moving as fast as anything," said the constable.

"Do you think he's a thief too?" Harry wanted to know.

"No doubt about it," said Mr. Narbut. "But look here, who was that man you were talking to in the woods last night? Wasn't Pym, was it?"

"Oh, no, sir," said Harry enthusiastically. "That's Mister Skatch. My friend. He has books for children. Good ones. Religious ones. He's come to help me."

"If he's like you say," agreed Mr. Narbut, "I'm sure you can trust him. 'Course boy, *I'm* your particular friend. And I'm not so sure it's right for you to stay here."

"I don't think my parents would want me to leave," suggested Harry. "They don't like me to go places."

"No, I don't want you to go against your parents," agreed Mr. Narbut reluctantly. "Still, something's got to be done. Tell you what: I'll fetch my rifle and come back and round them up. I suppose a boy like you could find a place to hide till I got back, couldn't you?"

"Yes, sir, I could," said Harry.

"Then go there till I get back," Mr. Narbut

told him. "If it's war they want, it's war they're going to get."

Giving the boy another pat on the head, the constable went out the gate and in his slow, plodding fashion pushed off toward town.

As soon as he was gone Harry went toward the barn, pausing to gather up some apples from the apple tree, stopping just to hurl a bad one at the ax. Once more he split the fruit in two.

In the barn he climbed into the hayloft and lay down, determined to stay there until Mr. Narbut returned. He knew he was perfectly hidden even if someone came near. Biting into an apple, he hoped the constable would arrest Miss Trowbridge. Then he would have the house to himself till his parents returned. It would be splendid.

He did wonder if Mr. Skatch would return. The truth of the matter was he didn't like the constable nearly as much as he did the colporteur. As far as Harry was concerned, Mr. Skatch was his *best* friend.

Thinking of that made Harry recall the book the colporteur had given him, *The Dangers of Dining Out*. Pulling it from his back pocket, he opened it to the flyleaf, to admire the fine hand in which Mr. Skatch had written his name. Then, with great pleasure, he turned to the section titled *Confessions of a Maniac*.

CHAPTER 22

MISS TROWBRIDGE AND MR. SMITH MAKE PLANS
· HARRY MAKES HIS PLANS ACCORDINGLY

M iss Trowbridge was so upset that she could not sit still. Up and down she went, around and about the house she walked until a pounding at the door brought her to a halt. When she unlatched the door, in came Mr. Smith—but I think we had best call him Mr. Pym now.

"It's gone," was the first thing that Miss Trowbridge said.

"What's gone?" asked a bewildered Mr. Pym.

"The Edgeworths' money box."

Having no notion what Miss Trowbridge was talking about, Mr. Pym attempted to calm her. First he made her sit down, then he took up a chair nearby and held her hand. "Explain yourself," he said gently.

As patiently as she could, Miss Trowbridge tried to tell him about the money box: that it had been left for her beneath the bed, that she was responsible for it, that she had just looked for it and—it was gone.

"Why were you even looking?"

"I haven't told you everything," she explained

reluctantly, becoming more and more upset. "Mister Narbut was here."

"Here?" cried Mr. Pym, who had no love for the man who had run him out of town.

Miss Trowbridge nodded. "He says Mister Edgeworth asked him to watch over the farm. He was about last night."

"Spying on us!" said Mr. Pym.

"He saw you," she continued, "though he didn't know it was you. He also saw the boy go out and talk to someone in the woods. Was it you?" she asked hopefully.

Mr. Pym shook his head.

"Mister Narbut wants to do me harm," she said after a moment.

"Why?"

She sighed. "Just a few days ago he asked me to marry him."

"He didn't!"

"I laughed at him."

"Did you tell him about us?" asked Mr. Pym.

"I didn't dare," she whispered. "I suppose he knows that too. When he left, he talked to the boy."

"There's a lot of talking to that boy, isn't there?"

"He's a good boy," said Miss Trowbridge vaguely.

"I bet it was that Mister Skatch he talked to last night," said Mr. Pym.

"He's a stranger," objected Miss Trowbridge. "He just came."

"He's built himself a regular lean-to in the woods, he has!"

"In the woods?" asked Miss Trowbridge. "Here?"

"I just saw it, didn't I?"

Miss Trowbridge became all of a heap again. "I never should have asked you to come," she said with a whimper. "You must go away. Mister Narbut will surely tell Doctor Williams, and it will be awful!" She covered her face with her hands at the mere thought of what might happen.

"I'm not going unless you come with me," said Mr. Pym stoutly, determined not to leave. "You're my wife," he said, with an attempt at tenderness.

Miss Trowbridge shook her head. "I have to take care of the boy. And the box, Nicholas," she added. "If it really is gone, they'll say I took it." Suddenly she drew herself up. "Get your things," she fairly ordered. "You've got to go."

Pushed by her insistence, Mr. Pym reluctantly went with her to the barn. Once there, he slowly began to gather up the few things that were his.

"Look here," said Mr. Pym after a few

moments. "I'll go. But I'm not going farther than I have to. If that fellow Skatch can hide in the woods, I suppose I can too."

"Please!" insisted Miss Trowbridge, stamping her foot impatiently. "You mustn't get into more trouble."

"I'm not going to leave you now," he returned. "Tell me a place to go, somewhere you can get to me quickly if you've the need. I'll give you my word: I'll not come unless you call."

Miss Trowbridge, too tired and agitated to argue, gave in. "Where is this Mister Skatch staying?" she asked.

"Not far off down along the road in the woods."

"Then go in the opposite direction," Miss Trowbridge told him. "There's a creek that feeds the pond out back. Follow it, and you'll come to a small waterfall. You can stay there, and I'll know where to find you. Only please, you must go now," she begged.

"I'm going," he reassured her, and they both hurried out of the barn.

Harry, who had been hiding in the hayloft, had of course heard everything the two had said in the barn. As soon as they left he scrambled down and looked out the window as the two embraced each other. Then Mr. Pym went one way while his wife returned to the house.

In an instant Harry made up his mind: He
would tell Mr. Skatch exactly where Mr. Pym was
hiding. Perhaps they could catch him. Wouldn't
that be larks!

CHAPTER 23

HARRY AND MR. SKATCH GO A-HUNTING ·
WHAT THEY CATCH

Hastily Harry ran to the woods where, having
heard what Mr. Pym had said, he knew he would
be able to find Mr. Skatch. Once there, he
shouted the colporteur's name, knowing that the
only one who could hear him would be his friend.
Sure enough, Mr. Skatch quickly came forward.

"He's gone off!" shouted Harry breathlessly as
soon as he saw the colporteur.

"Who has?"

"Mister Pym. The other thief!"

Taking Harry by the shoulders, Mr. Skatch
attempted to calm the boy. "Who is Mister Pym
and where did he go?" he asked.

"I was up in the hayloft, hiding," Harry
explained, "when Miss Trowbridge came in with
Mister Smith . . . only his real name is Mister

Pym. She told him he had to go away."

"Why was that?" asked Mr. Skatch.

"I don't know, sir, but she was all upset. She made him promise to go, but he didn't want to. Then she told him about the waterfall up the creek. And he went there. I'm telling the truth, sir, I am!"

"I'm sure you are," said Mr. Skatch kindly. "There isn't a more truthful, well-meaning boy in all creation."

"Don't you think, sir, we could catch Mister Pym?" suggested Harry.

"Catch him?"

"He won't be expecting us, and I can show you where he's hiding," urged Harry.

"Why do you want to do that for?"

"I don't like them," said Harry. "They haven't told the truth. Besides," he admitted, "it will be great fun."

Mr. Skatch took a moment to consider. "You *are* a brave lad, aren't you?" he said, bestowing his most splendid smile. "Perhaps we should catch him. Can you really show me the way so that he won't see us coming?"

"Just follow me," cried Harry.

"Wait one moment," said the colporteur. Leaving Harry, he hastened to his lean-to where, from the very bottom of his traveling bag, he pulled out a small revolver. He loaded the gun and dropped it into his jacket pocket, then returned to the excited Harry. "Now, lead the way!"

Off they started, Harry in the lead, plotting a wide circle in order to take Mr. Pym by surprise. More than once Mr. Skatch had to tell him to slow down. First they went down the Edgeworths' road. Then they turned toward Fairington.

A mile down that road, Harry, with Mr. Skatch prancing along, moved into the woods. Once there, they moved very much more slowly, pausing to stop, look, and listen every few yards.

As soon as they heard the waterfall, Harry made a sign. Mr. Skatch came forward. Much to Harry's surprise, the saintly soul drew a revolver from his pocket. But with a finger to his lips, Mr. Skatch pressed forward.

Poor Mr. Pym. He was doing no more than sitting on a rock puttering about his own thoughts, and he never noticed Mr. Skatch or Harry till it was too late.

"Please don't move!" commanded Mr. Skatch as he came right up behind the man.

"Got him!" cried Harry, dancing into the view of the astonished Mr. Pym. "We've got him!"

CHAPTER 24

WHAT HAPPENS TO MR. PYM · MR. SKATCH

WRITES A MOST CURIOUS SORT OF LETTER

It took Mr. Pym a moment to settle his thoughts. "Who," he finally asked Mr. Skatch, who was holding his pistol in such a way that it was clear that he would use it, "do you think you are?"

"A protector of children," returned Mr. Skatch sweetly, a smile illuminating his face. "Now please move in the direction I wish you to go. We must not remain here."

Harry, with growing excitement, saw that Mr. Pym did not wish to move. He watched Mr. Skatch carefully.

"Please," the colporteur said softly, but cocking the hammer of his gun as he spoke. "I've no desire to harm you—'Thou shall not kill'—but I will do so if you don't move."

Mr. Pym, impressed with the authority of Mr. Skatch's manner, reluctantly did as he was told. Harry was bid to lead the way, while Mr. Skatch, pistol in hand, followed behind Mr. Pym.

"Very good," said Mr. Skatch when they reached his lean-to. "Do you see that tree there?"

he asked Mr. Pym. "Sit down and straddle it with your arms and feet."

Reluctantly, Mr. Pym did as he was told even as Mr. Skatch slipped a rope out of his bag. "Here, boy," he said to Harry, handing him the pistol. "If he moves, just pull the trigger."

Harry, astonished, gripped the pistol rigidly with two hands, pointing it right at the prisoner, who, if anything, was more fearful of the boy than the man. The colporteur, meanwhile, tied Mr. Pym's wrists and then his feet around the tree until the poor man was trussed like a pig on a spit.

"What do you intend to do?" demanded Mr. Pym.

"I told you," said Mr. Skatch, taking back his gun, "I'm here to protect this small boy."

"You'll not harm my wife," pleaded Mr. Pym.

"Your *wife?*" asked Mr. Skatch. "Who, might I ask, is your wife?"

"Annie Trowbridge."

"She told me he was her brother," Harry reminded them, seeing this confession as just one more justification for what he was doing.

"Of course," said Mr. Skatch, "we don't know if he's telling the truth now, either. But you can be sure," he informed Mr. Pym, "she won't meet with any harm whatever she is. Nor more than you shall. At least as long as you stay here. Now, Harry, dear boy, we need to talk privately."

With a familiar arm about the boy's shoulder, Mr. Skatch led Harry out to the roadway.

"Shall we catch Miss Trowbridge too?" asked Harry, eager for new adventures.

"The first thing," said Mr. Skatch, "is for you to go back home. Get yourself something to eat. In a short while I shall come to stay. Then I can really protect you. Would you like that?"

"Oh, yes, sir, I would," Harry readily agreed. "We'll have so much fun. But, sir, what about Mister Narbut?"

"Who is Mister Narbut?"

"The constable," explained Harry. "He was at the house this morning too. Right after you. It was Mister Narbut who told me to hide so that he could fetch his rifle."

Instantly Mr. Skatch's smile faded. "A *constable* was at your home?" he wanted to know.

Harry became worried over the colporteur's reaction. "He's looking after me too. But I don't like him as much as you."

"And he's coming back?" said Mr. Skatch.

"He said so. I haven't done anything wrong, have I? Can't I trust him?"

"Children have to be careful to whom they speak," said Mr. Skatch thoughtfully, trying to

. . . the poor man was trussed like a pig on a spit.

decide what might have brought the law.

"I won't listen to anyone but you, sir," said Harry hastily. "I'll go now as you told me to."

"Do that, and be a good boy," said Mr. Skatch.

Harry started, then stopped. "What shall I do if Miss Trowbridge tries to run away?" he asked, determined to do things the way Mr. Skatch wanted.

"If she should try to leave? Why—just lift your window. That will be our signal. I'll be looking on and won't let her go," he assured the boy.

When Mr. Skatch was certain the boy had returned to the house, he went back to where Mr. Pym was tied.

"I don't think you'll be detained for more than a day," he said to the helpless fellow. "Just keep in mind that there's no point in your trying to get away. You won't get far: Everybody knows you're not to be trusted."

Mr. Skatch fetched one of his little books from his bag and carefully tore out a blank page—a thing he did with pleasure—and with book in hand tipped his hat to Mr. Pym and walked off.

He went only to the edge of the woods. There he sat himself down and with his back comfortably propped up against a tree kept his eyes upon the Edgeworth house.

He put his pistol back into his pocket and

exchanged it for a pencil. Using the blank piece of paper he wrote:

Dear Horatio:

I hope and trust you are well. Please trust my very good friend Mr. Jeremiah Skatch. I have been thinking it would be a good idea for you to take my money box and give it to him for safe keeping. It will be safest that way. Please do as I tell you. Your mother sends her love. Remember, Horatio, *do* as I tell you.

Your father,
Abraham Edgeworth

Mr. Skatch studied his composition. It was not, he reassured himself, so very bad, and it was quite the simplest way for him to get the box.

Folding the paper carefully, he placed it in his pocket and resumed his careful, patient watch on the house.

CHAPTER 25

MISS TROWBRIDGE MAKES A PAINFUL DECISION · SHE ALSO WRITES A LETTER · A DEPARTURE · A WINDOW

Though Miss Trowbridge was greatly relieved that she had gotten Mr. Pym to leave, she remained so upset that she could hardly keep herself still. All about the house she walked, picking things up only to put them down.

The cause of this great anxiety was the money box; she knew very well that if anything happened to it, she would be blamed, by Constable Narbut if no one else. It would be enough to ruin her, blighting her marriage as would nothing else.

Perhaps, she thought, Harry had moved it. She knew he was not supposed to know about it—or so Mrs. Edgeworth had told her—but he had been acting so strangely that perhaps there was a connection. And so she tried to think where, if he had taken the box, he might have put it.

Moving from room to room, she searched as best she could, but discovered nothing save a ball of dirty clothes and a sooty rock beneath the boy's bed. It meant nothing to her.

While searching the top floor she looked out the window and saw Harry coming out of the woods. Down the stairs she went.

When Harry saw her waiting for him at the door, he stopped, pulled his cap over his eyes, walked in, and did his best to ignore her by heading straight for the steps.

Miss Trowbridge called to him. "Horatio," she said, trying to sound as pleasant as possible, "can you tell me where your parents' money box might be?"

Without looking at her, Harry whispered, "I don't know," and charged up to his room, slamming his door behind him.

Though exasperated by Harry's manner, Miss Trowbridge made herself sit down and think. What, she asked herself, was this Mr. Skatch doing camping in the Edgeworths' woods? What did *he* know about her? And Constable Narbut, how could he be so mean as to do what *he* was doing? How had he even known the money box was missing? As for Horatio, why was *he* acting so badly toward her?

It took her a long time to make up her mind, but at last she did. She realized now that it had been wrong to invite Mr. Pym. But what was done was done. What remained of her duty was toward the boy. Burning with a zeal to do the proper thing, she fetched pen and paper and wrote:

Dear Mr. and Mrs. Edgeworth:

I beg of you to come home at once! I am greatly alarmed and in much difficulty about what to do. A strange man, a seller of children's books, is lurking about. Moreover, I must tell you the truth about myself. PLEASE COME HOME AT ONCE!

Sincerely yours,

Annie Trowbridge

The letter composed, Miss Trowbridge sealed it in an envelope, relieved that she was at last doing the right thing, no matter what the consequences.

As it was getting late in the day, she fetched bonnet and shawl and stood at the bottom of the steps. "Horatio!" she called. "I must go to town and post a letter. Please come with me!"

Harry, who had been lying on his bed, sat up but did not answer.

"Horatio!" called Miss Trowbridge. "We must go to town!"

When Harry refused to reply, she shouted, "Very well, I shall go myself."

Harry went to his window to see if she really was going—as he truly believed—to escape.

Sure enough, Miss Trowbridge stepped out of the house. There she paused, trying to decide whether or not to go the regular way or to the place where she believed Mr. Pym was hiding. Naturally she wanted to see him and tell him what she had done.

But as she stood there trying to make up her mind she heard a noise above. Looking up, she saw that Harry had *opened* his window and was peering down at her. That made up her mind. The last thing she wanted to do was even hint as to Mr. Pym's whereabouts. She would go the regular way by horse and cart.

After putting the horse and wagon in order, she set out, aware that Harry was watching her every move. On her part she absolutely refused to look back upon his surly critical face. All in all, she decided that he was a most unpleasant child. Oh, how she regretted ever having taken the position!

CHAPTER 26

IN WHICH MISS TROWBRIDGE HAS A MEETING WITH MR. SKATCH · ALSO, WHAT HAPPENS TO THE LETTER

Through the gate and along the rutted road briskly trotted the wagon; Miss Trowbridge held the letter in her hand with the reins. Caught up in her own thoughts, she let the horse have its own way, and so she was quite surprised to look up and find Mr. Skatch standing on the road blocking the path.

Taken aback by the colporteur's unexpected appearance, Miss Trowbridge's hands jerked upward, causing the letter to flutter to the bottom of the wagon. Snatching it, she attempted to hide it behind her back. Too late; Mr. Skatch had seen it.

Smiling, nodding in his most pleasant manner, Mr. Skatch approached the wagon and scratched

the horse pleasantly between its ears even as
—with his other hand—he gripped the bit to
prevent Miss Trowbridge from moving.

"Good afternoon, madam," he said politely.

"Afternoon," returned Miss Trowbridge, greatly alarmed.

"You were coming along so fast," he said, "and
in such deep thought that I decided you must be
in some distress. I hope and trust nothing is
amiss."

"No, nothing," replied Miss Trowbridge, her
heart fluttering.

"And the boy?" asked Mr. Skatch sweetly.
"Where is he?"

"At home," she replied, though even as she
spoke she wondered what compelled her to say
anything.

"Left alone?" inquired Mr. Skatch, one eyebrow
raised in a look of pained surprise. "Where, pray,
could you be going that you must leave such a
defenseless boy alone?"

Miss Trowbridge began to feel anger. "It can't
be any of your business," she suggested.

"Ah!" he cried. "But it *is* my business. I have an
interest in *everything* about children. They need
constant looking after."

Miss Trowbridge whispered, "I don't think you
are needed, sir."

"Please give me that letter you are holding," said Mr. Skatch abruptly. He held out one hand, while the other still firmly controlled the horse.

Frightened, realizing that she could neither run nor call for help, Miss Trowbridge reluctantly gave Mr. Skatch the letter. He took it, scanned the address, then let go of the horse. With a slip of his finger he opened the envelope.

Miss Trowbridge turned pale.

"Madam," he said with great care after he had read the note, "you are doing wrong. You and that dangerous man—that Mister Pym—are trying to lure the Edgeworths into a trap so as to steal *all* their money. That, as a gentleman and fighter against all sin, I must not, cannot, allow!"

So saying, he tore the letter into tiny bits and scattered them about. "Now then, no more letters!" So saying, he turned his back on the poor woman and marched into the woods until Miss Trowbridge lost sight of him.

CHAPTER 27

IN WHICH MISS TROWBRIDGE GOES FOR HELP · A CRUCIAL MEETING ALONG THE WAY · WHAT HAPPENS TO HER HOPES

Miss Trowbridge was so angry that she trembled. She was angry at herself. She was angry at Mr. Skatch. She was angry at the entire situation. Yet, what was she to do?

She wanted to rush off to town, but an acute sense of the danger in leaving the boy held her. At the very same time she reminded herself how clearly Harry had shown his dislike of her. There was nothing she could think of that might change his mind.

Then she considered that she had best find Mr. Pym. But alas, she was convinced that Mr. Skatch was hiding, watching, only waiting for her to lead him to her husband and all the dangers that implied. Had he not known her husband's name? No! She would not lead him to Mr. Pym.

In the end she made up her mind the only way she could: She would go to Constable Narbut and demand his help, no matter how unpleasant that might be. He was bound to give it. Gathering the reins, Miss Trowbridge urged the horse to town.

But the closer she got to Fairington, the more worried and anxious she grew about leaving Harry. How many times did she actually stop and think it all out again, coming to the conclusion that she must return to the Edgeworths' home? No sooner did she do that than the image of the suspicious face of the boy peering down on her from his open window bore upon her mind, and once again she moved toward town.

But Miss Trowbridge never reached Fairington. Half a mile before town she spied Mr. Narbut coming along on his horse, rifle in hand. He was not alone. To Miss Trowbridge's horror, Dr. Williams, her guardian, was with him.

The minister sat astride his piebald nag, his whitened head bobbing, his black jacket hanging like a flag without wind, his top hat like a cold, empty chimney. Even from the distance at which she first spied him she could see that Mr. Narbut had told all.

When the constable saw Miss Trowbridge, he stopped and bid the minister stop too, waiting for the young lady to come to them. This she did until, only a few yards away, she leaped from the wagon and ran to the constable's side.

"Mister Narbut," she cried, "you must come. I'm afraid something awful is going to happen."

Constable Seymour Narbut, cool in crises, did

not so much as flinch an inch, but sat tall upon his horse like a lord. "What's going to happen?" he asked.

His dry, suspicious manner made Miss Trowbridge pause, but having committed herself, she repeated what she had said. As for Dr. Williams, she dared not even look at him. The minister sat mutely by, his unhappy eyes fixed upon his ward.

After hearing her plea for the second time, Mr. Narbut merely said, "Where's the boy?"

"At the house."

"You say there's danger," he smirked, "yet you let the boy stay alone."

"He *wouldn't* come!" insisted Miss Trowbridge, as much to Dr. Williams as to Mr. Narbut. "Please, ask me whatever you like as we go, but please come!"

Mr. Narbut refused to budge. The truth was he was enjoying himself. Nor would Dr. Williams move; he was dipping deeper into a state of mournful shock.

"Miss Trowbridge," said Mr. Narbut, "I'm a man who likes to understand a thing thoroughly before I deal with it. I suggest we all go back to my office. Once there you can tell us everything that has happened, *everything*." He rather leered over the word "everything."

In desperation Miss Trowbridge turned to Dr. Williams. "Please, sir," she began. "The Edgeworths have a money box."

"Do they now?" called Mr. Narbut with a sarcasm. "You didn't wish to talk about *that* before."

"It was hidden beneath their bed," continued Miss Trowbridge to the minister, trying to ignore the constable's taunts.

"How do you know?" Mr. Narbut challenged.

"I was told so!" she snapped back at him.

"I'm not so certain that's the truth," suggested the upholder of justice.

"Annie, child," said Dr. Williams at last, "you must tell the truth."

"They trusted me!" the poor lady cried.

"Too trusting," suggested Mr. Narbut.

"*The box is gone!*" Miss Trowbridge finally burst out.

"Is it now?" said Mr. Narbut, with infuriating insinuation. "How do you know that?"

"I looked," said Miss Trowbridge in all honesty.

"What right, Annie," asked the minister, "do you have to be looking where Mister Edgeworth hides his money?"

It was then that Miss Trowbridge realized that there was nothing she could say or do to make either of the men believe her. Regretting that she had ever come to town, she spun about and started back for the wagon, determined to return to the house herself. But Mr. Narbut, quick when he wished to be, spurred up his horse and placed himself between the young lady and her wagon.

Miss Trowbridge, seeing that she was blocked, could only cry out in vexation. "Mister Narbut," she told him, "I came to town to mail a letter to the Edgeworths telling them they must return."

"So they must," agreed the constable. "You can be sure I've already done so. Where's your letter?"

"It was taken from me," said Miss Trowbridge, finding herself once more in a helpless position.

"By whom?"

"A Mister Skatch, a tract seller. He's been hiding about the house. I'm sure he's the one you saw last night. And he's the one who took the letter from me. He frightens me!"

"There!" cried Mr. Narbut triumphantly to Dr. Williams. "Didn't I tell you how wicked she was, accusing the very man who had befriended the boy, the religious fellow!"

"I don't believe he's anything of the kind," protested Miss Trowbridge.

"Annie, child," said the minister. "I know the man well. He's a good, pious man. Am *I* not able to judge such things?"

"As I see it," cut in Mr. Narbut, "it's all a

simple work: You say the box is gone. I say you and your friend took it. I saw *him* about the house last night. And who is this friend of yours? That good-for-nothing Nicholas Pym—that's who it is!"

"Annie, child," said Dr. Williams, his voice shaking with emotion, "Mister Narbut tells me that this Mister Pym was with you. That cannot, must not, be true."

Miss Trowbridge, absolutely furious, could no longer hold back the truth: "Mister Pym is my husband," she cried.

"*Husband!*" echoed Dr. Williams, aghast. "It's not possible. Without my permission? Without my blessing? Impossible. I know nothing about it!"

"There!" said Mr. Narbut triumphantly. "An illegal marriage. I always thought she was a likely one to break the law. I've an eye for it. I only held my tongue out of respect for you, Doctor Williams. I daresay," he continued, turning to Miss Trowbridge, truly enjoying himself, "that he's stolen the money and run off without you. I can't say I'm surprised."

"If I show you where he is," said Mrs. Pym—which is what I think we had best call her from now on—"if I bring you to him, right now, you could see for yourself he's no such person, and hasn't done any such thing. Would you believe me then?"

Mr. Narbut was not at all sure what parts of her story were true and what were not. What did he care? She had admitted enough to suit him. So he deferred to the minister. "What do you say, Doctor Williams?"

"Nothing," said that good man, wrapped up in his own sense of betrayal. "I must go home, alone." So saying, he turned his horse about and bent toward town.

Mrs. Pym and Mr. Narbut watched him go, both with different states of mind. Then the constable said, "Very well. Show me where he is. We'll see if he has the money box or no. But, mind, no trickery. I'll decide what to believe when I see him."

Mrs. Pym, stricken by Dr. Williams' abandonment, merely said, "Mister Pym is waiting at the little waterfall by the Edgeworths' home."

"I warn you," said Mr. Narbut, "I have my doubts. If this Pym—husband or not—is *not* there, I shall go twice as hard on you."

"Mister Narbut," returned Mrs. Pym with a voice steadied upon the rock of her devotion, "if Mister Pym is *not* there, you may believe *anything* you wish!"

Relieved at last that she had found a way to get

the constable to move, she climbed back onto the wagon. After first tying his horse to it, Mr. Narbut followed her and took a seat, rifle across his knee.

Mrs. Pym hurried the horse till they came to a place along the road that she judged to be close to the waterfall. From there the two of them walked into the woods, Mrs. Pym leading the way, Narbut coming after. More than once, she had to beg him to hurry.

"Now you'll believe me," said Mrs. Pym when they came within earshot of the waterfall. So saying, she stepped into the clearing with Mr. Narbut, rifle in hand, peering around her.

But no one was there at all. Only a few of Mr. Pym's belongings gave evidence that he had even been there.

"He *might* have been here," tittered Mr. Narbut, "but he's run off, hasn't he? With the money box, too, I'll guess."

Once, twice, three times Mrs. Pym called. For her efforts she received not so much as an echo.

"Well now," said Mr. Narbut with total triumph, "didn't you say I was to believe whatever I liked if he wasn't here?"

Mrs. Pym, bewildered, said nothing.

"Then," continued the constable, "I beg to inform you that you're under arrest for conspiring to steal the Edgeworths' money. We'll just move on to the house to make certain that all's well with the boy. For your sake, I hope he's safe."

Mrs. Pym, all her hopes tumbled down to absolutely nothing, could only do as she was told.

CHAPTER 28

HARRY'S DEAR FRIEND, MR. JEREMIAH SKATCH, BRINGS HIM AN IMPORTANT LETTER · WHAT HE DOES WITH IT

What happened to Harry when Mrs. Pym, letter in hand, made her fateful trip through the woods? Left alone, he set himself upon the front steps of the house, wondering whether she was going to escape or not. That she was trying to escape he had not the slightest doubt. Indeed, he was suddenly struck by the notion that she *had* found the box and was running away with it.

Up the steps he tore and, candle in hand, peered up into the chimney. He held the light just so, and could make out the edge of the box. Relieved, but still agitated, he returned to the front door and waited anxiously. When at last he saw Mr. Skatch emerge from the woods, Harry

was so glad to see him that he rushed forward
with a joyous whoop.

"Well then, my brave young man," said Mr.
Skatch in greeting. "I said I would come, and
here I am!" Graciously he allowed Harry to carry
his portmanteau through the gate. But once there
he paused. "Is Miss Trowbridge about?" he asked
in a whisper.

Harry was horrified. "Oh, sir, didn't you see
my signal?" he cried aghast. "She's gone. I opened
the window just like you told me."

"Don't worry," Mr. Skatch reassured him.
"Good riddance is what I say!"

"She wanted to know where the money box
was!" Harry informed him.

"The impudence!" said Mr. Skatch, clearly
shocked. "But I daresay," he ventured with a level
gaze of his bright blue eyes upon the boy, "you
were strong enough to refuse her that information."

"I did refuse, sir," replied Harry. "It's still just
where I put it. Did I do the right thing?"

Mr. Skatch, with the grandest of gestures,
dashed off his hat and bowed before the boy. "*Of
course* you did the right thing. You always do the
right thing. A brave, wise lad. I defy the man
who says otherwise. I for one would trust you
with anything!"

Harry's heart nearly swelled to bursting, he felt so proud at these words. "But what about Mister Pym, sir? What shall we do about him?"

"Not to worry," said Mr. Skatch grandly. "By and by we shall do something. You see, it depends, doesn't it, on where Miss Trowbridge has gone. But there, I've just remembered. I had to go to town—no doubt that's why I missed your signal—and stopped at the post office. The Children's Protective Society needs to know where I am. The postmaster asked me to bring this to you." From his pocket he drew the letter he himself had written and handed it over to Harry. "It's from your parents."

Harry, delighted, took the letter eagerly, reading it right away. But as he did his joy quickly faded. What was the matter? Had not Mr. Skatch *just* told him how wise, how trustworthy, smart, and capable he was? He had. Yet here was a letter from Harry's father—for so he supposed it to be—suggesting that he was none of those things, that his parents did *not* trust him to take care of the money box. It made Harry's resentment rise up again.

"What do they say?" inquired Mr. Skatch casually. "Are they in good health? Is everything well with their trip?"

Poor Harry. He felt too ashamed to tell Mr.

Skatch what the letter revealed lest that good friend learn his parents' low opinion of him. So, instead of answering Mr. Skatch's question, he merely said, "They wish me well," and unceremoniously shoved the letter into his back pocket, avoiding Mr. Skatch's puzzled eyes.

Mr. Skatch had reason to be puzzled. Vexed with the boy for not telling him what the letter had said, he felt stymied about how to get the box from him. But even as he was trying to consider the matter, Mrs. Pym, followed by Constable Narbut, appeared from around the back of the house.

CHAPTER 29

IN WHICH MRS. PYM IS GIVEN ALL SHE DOES NOT DESERVE · MR. SKATCH MAKES AN ARRANGEMENT · FINALLY, A HYMN OF PRAISE THAT CONTAINS A FEW WORTHY SENTIMENTS

The appearance of Mrs. Pym and Mr. Narbut revealed a great contrast. Mrs. Pym, not sixteen years of age, walked bowed, like an old woman. Her face was ashen, her eyes dull. She fairly stumbled as she came. Mr. Narbut strutted tall and proud, like a rooster in its prime.

When the constable saw Harry, he went right over to the boy and began to pump his hand in congratulations. "Good for you," he crowed. "I should have known you could manage on your own. Your father will be proud of you!" He nodded toward Mr. Skatch. "Who is this gentleman?" he asked in a low voice.

The colporteur was not a man to wait for introductions. "Mister Jeremiah Skatch at your service, sir," he announced. "Purveyor of moral instruction to American youth on behalf of the Children's Protective Society. A particular friend of the Edgeworths. An even more particular friend of brave Harry. Willing friend of the famous Constable Narbut, known to all the world as a man who labors with skill, purpose, and dedication."

Mr. Narbut, who was inclined to share these sentiments, looked to Harry for confirmation.

"It's true," Harry offered proudly. "He is my friend."

Mr. Narbut turned, looking from Mr. Skatch to Mrs. Pym. "And *that* man," he said to her, "is the man you accused!"

Mrs. Pym, too miserable, looked but said nothing.

"She accused you, sir," Mr. Narbut informed

Mr. Skatch, "of being a danger, a thief. Claims you tore up some letter of hers!"

"Did she!" cried Mr. Skatch, whose features registered scandal even as his fingers touched his heart. "The girl must not be believed!"

"I thought as much," agreed Mr. Narbut with easy glee. He turned to Harry. "Have you seen the man she claims is her husband, Mister Pym?"

Harry looked to Mr. Skatch for guidance.

"Go on," urged the modest Mr. Skatch to the boy: "*You* did it, not I."

Alarmed, Mrs. Pym looked up.

"Did what?" questioned Mr. Narbut.

"This boy," proclaimed Mr. Skatch, stepping in before Harry could speak, "this *brave* young man actually captured Mister Pym lurking about the woods whilst he was thinking heaven only knows what thoughts. Caught him, tied him up, and has him nice and neat not far from here."

Mr. Narbut whistled. "Is that a fact?"

"Oh, I helped a trifle," admitted Mr. Skatch with careful pride. "But it was far and away the boy's doing, not mine."

"Well, then," said Mr. Narbut, hastening to stake his claim, "I've arrested the woman."

"What for?" asked Mr. Skatch.

"Stealing from the Edgeworths."

"I did no such thing," cried Mrs. Pym with a burst of indignation.

"Then," said Mr. Narbut with a wag of his head, "I suppose the money box disappeared all by itself."

Harry, becoming nervous, said nothing.

"I don't know what happened to it," repeated the hapless Mrs. Pym. "But I did not take it."

"Well," agreed Mr. Narbut who had no great interest in fine points of law or fact, "if you didn't take it, your so-called husband did, and that amounts to the same thing as far as I'm concerned."

"Do I understand you correctly," said Mr. Skatch. "Is the Edgeworths' money box gone?"

"Admits it herself," confirmed Mr. Narbut.

Now Harry, who was standing off to one side, was following this conversation but was not at all sure what to say. What had happened was no more than what he had hoped. Moreover, he was certain now that the Pyms had *wanted* to take the money box. Besides, he did not like them, and they had toyed with him, played tricks on him; obviously they deserved to be punished.

As he was thinking these thoughts he heard Mr. Skatch say, "The boy had a letter from his parents."

"Good," said Mr. Narbut. "I wrote to them to tell them they ought to come right home."

"Did you?" inquired Mr. Skatch with more than casual interest. "When did you do that?"

"Just this morning," Mr. Narbut informed him. "They should have the letter by now. You'll see them return in a hurry."

"Mister Narbut," said Mr. Skatch with sudden urgency, "what shall be done? Clearly, the woman is not fit to stay with the boy? Then there's Mister Pym in the woods."

"Show me where he is, and I'll bring them both back to town," suggested Mr. Narbut. "As for the boy, I'll mind him till the Edgeworths get back."

"You have been put through trouble enough," said Mr. Skatch sweetly. "You say it won't be long before his parents—my dear friends—come back. Let me stay here with the boy."

"Very handsome of you, Mister Skatch. What do you say to that, boy?"

Harry, still staring at Mrs. Pym, was deep in contemplation. He had not, in fact, ever seen anyone look so sad. "What will you do with Miss Trowbridge?" he ventured, something beginning to stir within his heart.

"Wants to be known as Mistress Pym," Mr.

Narbut informed him with a wink. "Whatever her name is, don't you worry your head. She'll be in jail."

"Will you put Mister Pym in jail too?" asked Harry.

"Soon as you show me where he is."

"Right this way!" called Mr. Skatch on cue. He had been watching Harry carefully and was eager to move apace. Indeed, he led the way so smartly that Harry, trudging in the rear, was given no opportunity to speak again.

There was, I'm sure you'll be glad to know, a touching reunion of Mr. and Mrs. Pym, who clung together despite the mocking eyes of Mr. Narbut, the censorious eyes of Mr. Skatch, and the wondering eyes of Harry.

"Off with them!" fairly commanded Mr. Skatch after Mr. Narbut had arrested Mr. Pym. Hand in hand, the unlucky couple moved off, followed at a safe distance by Mr. Narbut, gun at the ready, lest his captives try desperate acts.

"Hurrah!" cheered Mr. Skatch as the trio marched off down the road. "Justice is ever done!" And he put a strong, protective hand on Harry's shoulder. Pulling him firmly about, he guided him back toward the house, all the while triumphantly singing:

Hand in hand the unlucky couple moved off . . .

"How doth the little busy bee
Improve each shining hour,
And gather honey all the day
From every opening flower.

In works of labor or of skill
I would be busy too;
For Satan finds some mischief still
for idle hands to do!"

CHAPTER 30

A STARTLING CHANGE OF EVENTS

The remaining part of the afternoon was spent happily. Harry felt truly liberated and ran about with freedom and abandon. Mr. Skatch went along with him, complimenting him at every turn, altogether making the boy forget any misgivings that might have remained from the day's events.

When the afternoon had passed, the two returned to the house where supper was put together. Harry had the pleasure of watching the colporteur eat two whole chickens, eight slices of cold meat, twelve pickles, six pieces of whole corn, and one large pumpkin pie (plus coffee and cream to wash it down), all the while relating his adventures on the road. By the time Mr. Skatch had eaten his cheese and apple, Harry was convinced that he was the best human in all the world, worthy of respect and veneration.

Supper done, Mr. Skatch requested that he be shown the house. Harry was happy to oblige. But as it turned out, he could not show the colporteur enough. The more he saw, the more Mr. Skatch became excited, asking if there was anything else worth seeing.

Harry showed him the room behind the kitchen. "That's where Miss Trowbridge sleeps," he said.

"No more," Mr. Skatch assured him.

Harry almost felt sorry again, but seeing that Mr. Skatch wanted to hear nothing of that, they went up the steps.

"This is my parents' room," said Harry, leading the way.

Mr. Skatch observed it with minute care before he was willing to move on.

"My room," said Harry.

Mr. Skatch studied the room for what was—to Harry—an astonishingly long time. But again they left, and Harry showed him the remaining room, a small one off the hall. "This is the guest room," he pointed out.

Again Mr. Skatch scrutinized it with the same care he had lavished on the other rooms. His face was even more brilliantly animated than before, heightened by a thin film of sweat upon his brilliant brow, which caught the candlelight and made it seem to glow.

Turning, Harry began to go down the hallway, saying, "I think I've shown you everything, Mister Skatch."

Mr. Skatch remained standing outside the guest room. "Harry," he called.

Harry stopped and turned about.

"It's not *quite* everything," he said in a sepulchral tone that made the boy look at him curiously.

"Sir?" he said, puzzled.

"You have neglected one thing, one *very* important thing. Come now, dear boy, where in heaven's name did you put that money box?" His face as he spoke was one smile: Never was sun so bright.

Harry, taken by surprise, only looked at the man.

"What I mean to say," continued Mr. Skatch, measured but firm, "is this: Don't you think that

I—your protector—should know where you put it? After all, I'm not here *just* to protect you. I am here to protect that box. Why, what would happen if one of those desperate, angry, evil people—the Pyms—should break loose from the constable and return here to wreak their horrid vengeance on poor you? What would happen then, my dear boy?"

Harry, not fully understanding what Mr. Skatch was driving at, said nothing at all.

Nonetheless, Mr. Skatch waited for an answer. When none was forthcoming, he beckoned Harry to draw closer by wiggling a finger at him.

Harry came forward.

When he drew close, Mr. Skatch bent down so that Harry could feel the heat of the man upon his own face and sense his bad breath. "You did tell me, did you not," whispered Mr. Skatch, "that *you* placed that box in a *safe* place?"

"Yes sir, I did do that."

"And," continued Mr. Skatch sweetly, "it is still *exactly* where you put it, is it not? That is to say, you did not put it back where your father put it, under the bed?"

Harry uttered a breathless, "No."

With a sudden movement Mr. Skatch took Harry by the shoulders. "Please look me straight in the eyes when you speak to me," he commanded. "Now then, little boy. I shall repeat my question this once, and *only* once. You told me," he continued, his grip growing tighter and tighter, "that it was *still* hidden where you had placed it."

"Yes, sir," replied Harry in a small voice.

Mr. Skatch had begun his question with his usual smile. But, as Harry replied, that smile, like a sun in eclipse, began to fade away. And when Mr. Skatch spoke again it was slow, careful, and very quiet, for he wanted Harry to understand his every word. "Little boy," he said, his voice all but a whisper, "are you saying to me that you actually knew where the box was even while Mister Narbut was accusing that poor unfortunate simple girl of stealing it?"

Harry, completely bewildered by this change in Mr. Skatch, but understanding the import of the question only too well, could only nod.

"In other words," said Mr. Skatch, in tones so heavy they all but suffocated the boy and made it hard for him to breathe, "in other words, *you* allowed the constable to believe a *lie!*"

Harry could not even begin to speak.

"*Say something!*" commanded Mr. Skatch.

"Yes, I did," managed Harry, even as he jumped.

"*Thou* shalt not lie!" screamed the colporteur.

"*Thou* shalt not bare false witness!" And he shoved Harry away from him as if he were some horrible, loathsome, slimy thing.

"Poor woman," lamented Mr. Skatch. "Wicked, *wicked* boy!" Each time he said the word "wicked" it was as if he struck Harry bodily, it pained the boy so. Not that Mr. Skatch stopped. No, that righteous man went on. "If I had known," he continued, "but I thought you were a decent, honest, pious boy. What shall your parents say to this?"

Harry was so completely stunned by this turnabout in the man he considered his friend that he could not so much as move his tongue.

"Have you *nothing* to say for such shameful behavior?" demanded Mr. Skatch.

"I don't know," whispered the bewildered Harry.

"Doesn't know. Doesn't know!" Mr. Skatch repeated scornfully, sweeping about as if he were addressing an audience of thousands. "The boy sends innocent men and women to prison and says he doesn't know!" Mr. Skatch looked down upon Harry as if he had never seen so detestable a creature in all his life, and now, having seen one, wanted only to squash it.

"But, sir," pleaded Harry. "I told you so!"

"I lie!" roared Mr. Skatch. "I cheat! I, who

represent the Children's Protective Society? How dare you say such things? How dare you even *think* them! Now," he said, pointing an accusing finger at Harry, "now—*instantly*—fetch me that box so I may give it to the constable. Let us only hope that he doesn't put you in jail for the rest of your wicked life!"

Not believing what he was hearing, Harry could only repeat the words, "Fetch the box?"

"At once!"

"But—I—can't."

"Why not?"

"I—I—I don't want to."

"What possible reason is there for that ignorant decision?"

"You knew what I had done," insisted Harry, his tears beginning to fall.

"Then," screamed Mr. Skatch, "I shall have to find it for myself!" Turning about, he rushed into Harry's room and began to turn everything upside down. Harry, looking on from the doorway, watched, appalled, as Mr. Skatch threw over the bed and began to rip things from the trunk. It was as if the room were being broken to pieces. And when Mr. Skatch found nothing, he rushed out past the boy, knocking him aside as he flew down the steps.

Harry, dazed by what had happened, stumbled

into his room, shut the door, and tried to keep
from crying. Flinging himself upon the bed, he
grabbed a pillow and pushed his face into it,
trying to understand what had happened. From
below he heard horrendous crashings as Mr.
Skatch continued his rampaging search for the
box.

CHAPTER 31

IN WHICH HARRY MAKES AN ASTONISHING DISCOVERY

Harry still not only believed in Mr. Skatch but
he wanted to keep believing in him. Why should
he not? Had Mr. Skatch done anything wrong?
Not that Harry saw. For the moment, Harry's
great anxiousness had to do with Mrs. Pym. Had
he done her wrong?

Lying there on his tumbledown bed in his
thoroughly broken-up room, Harry tried to go
over in his mind what the woman had done, still
certain that she had done *something,* that she was
guilty in *some* way or another. Why else, he asked
himself, had he detested her so?

Had anything truly happened?

He searched and he searched, and to his amazement he found the answer to be—no.

Gradually it began to work through his mind that because he had been left behind he had become angry, angry at Mrs. Pym for being his jailer rather than at those who had made the law.

Then he thought about Mr. Skatch and tried to understand why that man had changed so much. It wasn't fair, he told himself. Hadn't he, Harry, told Mr. Skatch what he had done? When they had met in the woods the night before, he was sure he had. But then, he was forced to admit, he had lied to Mr. Narbut.

So it was not long before he began to think that he should fetch the money box and give it to the colporteur as he had demanded.

Thinking of the money box made him recall his father's letter. Why was it, he wondered, that no one ever trusted him to do anything right?

Still, the letter was a comfort. It reminded him of happier times. He took it from his pocket and held it open, glad just to have it with him. Trying to smooth out its many wrinkles, he read through it over and again. Though he didn't like what it told him to do, it made him feel better—he wasn't sure why himself.

Perhaps, he kept chiding himself, perhaps he should do what his father had told him to do, that is, give up the box to Mr. Skatch. Perhaps then the colporteur would not think him so bad.

Thinking very hard, Harry at last decided that he would do as his parents told him—give the box to Mr. Skatch. It would, after all, be the best thing.

Still, he found himself lacking the courage to do it. Instead, he lay there, admiring the handwriting of the letter. It was very elegant. It was, now that he studied it, much more fancy than he had recalled his father's writing to be. Where, he asked himself, had he seen his father's writing before?

Then he remembered: It was in *A Kiss for a Blow,* the book his parents had given him as a goodbye gift. His father had written something in that.

Hurriedly Harry got up, and after some frantic searching, uncovered the book from beneath the bedding. He opened it. There, just as he recalled, was his father's writing:

To Our Precious Little Horatio
A gift from his loving father and mother,
Mr. and Mrs. Abraham Edgeworth
October 1, 1845 A.D.

Puzzled, Harry placed the book with its open inscription side by side with the letter. He saw it at once: The book inscription and the letter were *not* written by the same hand.

For a long time Harry stared at the two specimens of writing, as if just by looking at them he could make them the same. He wanted them to be the same. He needed them to be the same. Yet he knew without question that they were not the same.

What made it worse was that he had *seen* his father write in the gift book. But since his father wrote the inscription, he wondered, who then wrote the letter? His mother? That didn't seem right. She would have put her name to it if she had. He knew that.

Then he thought that perhaps someone else wrote it because his father was sick. That, he forced himself to see, was not likely either. Suddenly a new thought came to him: How could his father tell him to give over the money box? *He, Harry, was not supposed to know about it!*

The more Harry looked at the two hand styles, the more he thought of what the letter said, the more he did not want to know the answer. Alas, there was no help for it.

Slowly, very slowly, he took from his pocket the little book *The Dangers of Dining Out* that Mr. Skatch had given him that morning. With trembling fingers he opened it and looked at the inscription the colporteur had written. There couldn't be any doubt: The inscription was in the same hand that wrote the letter.

Though Harry had not moved an inch, he felt as if he had been transported a million miles, to a world he had never seen before.

Once again, he forced himself to think of all that had happened. *Everything.* The more he did, the more upset he became, for it became clearer and clearer that Mrs. Pym had done nothing to him, nothing at all. Mrs. Pym had lied about Mr. Pym, but that was all. Perhaps, he found himself thinking, she had not even wanted the box.

No, they had *not* wanted it. It was something *he* had made up.

Understanding that, seeing what he had done, he saw what a really wicked child he had been. But even that self-accusation was nothing compared to the more important question he faced: What was he to do now?

The truth was, he was too fearful to ask the final question, the question about Mr. Jeremiah Skatch of the Children's Protective Society. That question was: Could Mr. Skatch be a fraud? Could *he* be a thief?

Harry lay there thinking all these things till his head hurt. He thought so long and so hard that he fell asleep. When he awoke, there was sunlight streaming in through the window. He had slept right through the night.

Now that Harry was awake, there was but one question in his mind: Had Mr. Skatch found the money box?

CHAPTER 32

WHAT HAS HAPPENED TO THE UNLUCKY PYMS? · AND HOW HAS IT AFFECTED CONSTABLE NARBUT?

Constable Seymour Narbut, the fury of Fairington, had marched Mr. and Mrs. Pym smartly down the road until he reclaimed the Edgeworths' wagon. With his rifle ever at the ready, he made Mr. Pym drive them into town in grand fashion. Roman generals did not exhibit captured emperors with greater pride than he.

Taking no chances with such dangerous persons, he clapped them safely into the one cell that Fairington could call its own. With a final, "Now don't go away," he left them.

It was Constable Seymour Narbut's finest hour. And he could no more keep his exploits from the world than he could stop admiring his talents. He

went to the tavern and told his tale there. He
went to the post office, and perhaps thinking that
from that spot it would speed round the world,
repeated the story. He went to the general store
and revealed it yet again, lovingly telling each and
every desperate detail, all that had occurred, as
well as some that did not.

Listening to Constable Narbut tell the adven-
ture, people just knew—he said so himself—that
he was the smartest, bravest, cleverest man in all
of Fairington Township, perhaps in the state,
quite possibly in the Union. Mr. Narbut never
did believe in false modesty, or in any other kind
of modesty for that matter. True, he had only
done his duty, but he had done it better than any
other man had done, would do, or might do. He
was not the least bit shy about that.

He even searched out Dr. Williams. That was
not easy. Truly, it gave Mr. Narbut pause. But he,
as we have seen, was never one to shrink from
unpleasant truth. He told the poor minister the
entire story from start to finish as only a brave
man could tell it. So honest was he in his telling
that he left out only one small fact; to wit, that he
had been in love with Miss Trowbridge, asked her
to marry him, and that she had refused him with
a laugh. But, as he knew from the depths of his
soul, that had absolutely nothing to do with the case.

"I'm sorry for your sake," he told Dr. Williams. "But I took my oath to protect people, and everything—personal feelings, all that rubbish —goes before that."

Dr. Williams' tears, white against white, were not noticed.

That night, crowds gathered around the little jail. They whooped, they hollered, they tried to peer into the cell through its one small window; and in every way they made things unpleasant for the Pyms. It became so bad that Mr. Pym felt obliged to hang his jacket over the window. This was a true disappointment to the crowd and created general bad feelings all around.

Mr. Narbut took his seat before the jailhouse, accepting congratulations, explaining yet once again and again how he did this, that, and the other thing. It was not until a good while into the evening that someone bothered to ask him about the Edgeworths' small boy.

"Oh, him," returned Mr. Narbut easily. "Nothing to worry about. He's being taken care of by the Edgeworths' best friend, a fellow by the name of Jeremiah Skatch, don't you know. He's the religious fellow. Puts up books for children. Doctor Williams thinks the world of him."

After a while the crowd, becoming bored, began to dwindle. Even Mr. Narbut became tuckered out and finally went to seek his dinner before yet another audience. He felt good. He had done his job. Above all, he reminded himself —and wasn't it the most important thing of all?—the boy was protected.

CHAPTER 33

MR. SKATCH DOES AN UNEXPECTED THING

It was the dazzling October light that woke Harry that next morning. His first inclination, being in a kind of stupor, was to shut his eyes and go back to sleep. Then, like a bubble bursting on a placid pond, he suddenly remembered where he was, what had happened, and most of all what might have happened: Had Mr. Skatch found the money box?

He sat up and listened, not at all sure what he expected to hear. Perhaps nothing. When no sounds came, he began to think that Mr. Skatch was gone. That, he knew, was not necessarily a good thing, no, not if he had found and taken the money box. Then, directly below his room, came the crash and crunch of crockery.

Mr. Skatch was still about.

Harry crept to his door, opened it a wee bit, and listened. All he could tell was that Mr. Skatch was walking about. From time to time there came sounds of more breakage. It was clear enough what was happening: The colporteur was still looking for the money box.

Harry went back to his bed and lay upon it. Though he was frightened, he knew he had to do something. For a while he toyed with the idea of running away. But he felt a real responsibility for what had happened, and was determined beyond all else to protect the money box.

As time passed and nothing actually happened, his fear began to fade. It was replaced by anger, anger that Mr. Skatch had tricked him by appearing to be on his side. Even so, Harry made himself remember that he had accused others wrongfully. Perhaps he was wrong about Mr. Skatch.

A particularly loud crash from below made Harry sit up. He returned to his door, looked out, then returned to his bed and lay down on it. Sooner or later he knew that Mr. Skatch would come.

Despite his best intentions, Harry had begun to doze off when footsteps right outside his door drove him to the top of wakefulness again. Not wanting, or rather not daring, to look at Mr.

Skatch, Harry turned over on his stomach and stared at the floor. The door opened.

"You're not still asleep, are you?" asked Mr. Skatch.

Harry did not answer.

"I would have thought you were at your prayers," said the colporteur.

Still Harry did not answer.

"I have been looking for that box," said Mr. Skatch, weariness thickening his voice. "When I find it, do you know what I intend to do with it?"

Harry remained mute.

"I shall bring it directly to Constable Narbut," he informed Harry. "He shall let those poor innocent people go. Then I'm very certain he will come for you. I shudder to think of your punishment."

Though Harry remained still, his heart beat so loudly that he was afraid Mr. Skatch would hear it.

Instead, Mr. Skatch only came farther into the room and looked down at the boy. Harry heard him sigh. "Now," he said, attempting to find the proper kindly voice range that Harry had heard so often before, "even though I should not, I will make a bargain with you: If you show me where the box is, and do it quickly, we shall just take it to town, you and I. I will personally beg Mister

Narbut not to be too hard on you. I shall even pray for you," he said, in his final, most generous offer.

Harry did not reply.

Waiting, Mr. Skatch's eyes—eyes now as red from exhaustion as was his flaming beard —scanned the room. The letter he had written, the one supposedly from Harry's father, lay on the floor right next to an open book, *A Kiss for a Blow*. Near it was his own gift, *The Dangers of Dining Out*.

Suddenly he realized what Harry had done. With a step forward, he attempted to pick up the letter, but Harry, aware of what Mr. Skatch was about to do, swung around and snatched both books and letter into his arms.

Mr. Skatch, caught by surprise, stepped back. The two looked at each other.

Harry began to breathe hard. "You're nothing but a thief," he said, sniffling back some sobs. "You tricked me and made me think wrong things about Miss Trowbridge. That letter wasn't from my father. You wrote it. *You* want to steal the money box!"

Mr. Skatch, in spite of himself, smiled. "I beg to inform you that you had your own thoughts regarding the young lady. As for the rest . . ."

He paused for a moment. "Perhaps I had better leave."

Harry, not daring to trust anything the man said, only watched as Mr. Skatch turned about and went down the hall and steps.

From his window, Harry watched the colporteur step outside. Wearing his jacket and high hat, carrying his portmanteau, Mr. Skatch gave every indication that he was in fact going. Harry felt so good seeing the man leave that he all but giggled.

As Mr. Skatch reached the front gate he paused and looked back at Harry's window. It made the boy's joy ebb away. But then, once more, Mr. Skatch continued to stalk up the path, away from the house, and toward the woods.

Harry, so happy that he skipped, was about to run downstairs when he made himself stop. Might Mr. Skatch be tricking him? Back to the window he ran. No, there was no more doubt in his mind: Mr. Skatch was moving with all deliberate speed toward the woods.

CHAPTER 34

AN ASTONISHING TURN OF EVENTS!

To talk about a weight being lifted from shoulders misses by far. Rather, think of the great god Atlas being allowed to put aside the entire Earth, which he had been carrying these many years. Then you might begin to think how Harry felt.

As for the dizziness, that quickly passed as he sat down on his bed to decide what he should do next. It did not take long: He would get the money box, bring it to Constable Narbut, confess how wrong he had been, tell him all about what Mister Skatch truly was, and beg the constable to let the Pyms out of jail. Finally, and most importantly of all, he intended to offer to go to jail himself.

How good it made Harry feel just to think it was possible for him to do all those *good* things. It brought tears of relief to his eyes. And maybe, a small inner voice said to him, maybe he would not have to go to jail because he had confessed all his sins.

Though he knew the house was empty—and what a curious feeling that was—Harry walked carefully down the hall toward his parents' room. It was a terrible sight: Everything had been overturned—bed, chest, chairs, even parts of the floor had been ripped up. Mr. Skatch had searched everywhere. It made Harry ill to see it.

Feeling a slight tremor at the renewed thought of the man and his violence, Harry went to the window and looked out to see if there was any sign of the colporteur. None.

Stepping boldly into the fireplace, Harry looked up. Unfortunately, without a candle, all he could see was the bright blue morning sky above, as if he were looking through the wrong end of a telescope. What is more, he could see no sign of the box.

In the grip of unease, Harry decided that he had best find out if the box was still there. Reaching one hand high, he began to pull himself up, using his legs as he had done before.

With a sharp kick he moved into the flue. Soot cascaded down. Pressing his knees outward to brace himself, he moved slowly but nonetheless upward. It was his legs, pressing outward, that kept him steady. Reaching again as high as he could, he tried to feel for the ledge where he had placed the box.

But it was not there. At least, it was not where he remembered it should be.

Harry looked up again, and fighting to keep his panic down, considered that perhaps he was not reaching in the right direction. He tried yet another side. Still he found nothing.

Fear flooded in on him.

Perhaps, he told himself, he was still not high enough. With another shove, and more pushing and more pulling, he moved higher yet another few feet.

Once that much farther along, he stretched as high as he could, still using his knees to keep from falling back. With his fingers extended to their greatest length, his back aching from the strain, he touched the box.

It was, after all, exactly where he had put it, only farther up than he had recalled.

If he had been flooded with fear before, now he was flooded yet again, but with relief. He *would* take the box down and bring it to Constable Narbut.

Easing himself up just a little bit higher, Harry lay the flat of his hand against the box, feeling for the latch and lock. They, too, were there. The box was intact.

Only then did Harry truly relax. Dropping his hand, he simply looked up, staring high into the sky through the chimney top that was some six feet above his head. He closed his eyes. Darkness provided more comfort.

Then, like a tickle in his ear, he heard a sound from below, the sound of one step, then another. He had to bite his lips to keep from crying out. For he knew as well as if it had been announced that Mr. Jeremiah Skatch was moving about in his parents' room. Once more, Harry had been fooled. And oh, he knew it too!

"Very well, my helpless Harry," came the soothing sweetness of Mr. Skatch, who spoke with utter calm. "I know you are up there. Now, let us end all this fuss. Bring that money box down to me."

CHAPTER 35

WHAT HELPLESS HARRY DID

Looking down, Harry could see the brown tips of Mr. Skatch's shoes. Looking up, he could see nothing but the sky.

"Do come down," said Mr. Skatch, continuing in a pleasant vein. "I shan't hurt you. All I desire is that box. Nothing more."

Harry pushed his back against the chimney flue, not daring to move one way or another or utter so much as a word.

"Dear boy," continued Mr. Skatch, his anger beginning to show, "must I really come and get you?"

Harry looked down and watched as Mr. Skatch leaned over and looked up. His face was very strange to see thus—nostrils flaring; neck reddish, raw, and bristling; eyes white. It was enough to make certain Harry's resolve *not* to go down. No, he would not.

That left him with no other way to go but up. As far as he was concerned, there was no choice in the matter. First, however, he had to get the box.

In itself, that proved to be no difficulty. Edging himself up a few more inches he pulled the box from its crevice with an easy motion. Slight and light, he settled it under one arm.

Pushing his back against the flue, Harry reached out and took hold of a projecting stone, one that was sticking out, hoping to use it as a handle to pull himself up. For his effort, all that happened was that the stone dropped out of the wall and fell, narrowly missing him. It also just missed Mr. Skatch.

That gentleman let out a roaring howl of rage, certain that Harry had purposely dropped the

"Fool!" he cried. *"Idiot! Do you* want *me to come after you?"*

stone in order to break open his head. "Fool!" he cried. "Idiot! Do you *want* me to come after you?"

As Mr. Skatch, his temper quite lost, attempted to squeeze his bulk into the hearth, Harry was not at all sure that big as he was, Mr. Skatch would not be able to follow. Not that he waited to see. Putting his hand in the hole left by the fallen stone, Harry hauled himself up still farther.

Mr. Skatch, with growing anger, began swearing violent oaths as he struggled to follow. For a long moment, Harry was sure the colporteur would actually do it. As Mr. Skatch reached up and snapped and snatched at Harry's feet with his fingers, intent on dragging the boy down bodily, Harry began to kick furiously with one foot and at the same time claw himself higher. Fortunately he found another grip, one that held: Farther up he moved.

Below, Mr. Skatch had wedged himself inside the chimney, but he proved much too great for it and could only manage to lift one arm. Nonetheless, Harry could feel the man's fingers flicking at his heels, like the lapping tongue of a dog (or wolf, I should rather say). Then, worse yet, he felt Mr. Skatch actually clutch a foot. In a burst of fright, up went Harry, losing one shoe to the demoniac man below.

"Down, damn you!" shouted Mr. Skatch, who had to be content with the one shoe.

I need hardly tell you that Harry had absolutely no desire to stop there. Feeling over his head, he found yet another hold, pressed his back against the wall, and moved up some more. The truth is, he wanted to reach the sky. If an angel had reached down a helping hand, Harry, without so much as a "Who are you?" would have gleefully gripped it.

The problem was, that the farther Harry went up the chimney, the narrower it became. The walls felt as though they were pushing in at him, squeezing him in a rough, cold, hard embrace. If ever his smallness was a blessing, it was at that moment and in that chimney. Harry knew it and was glad.

He looked below. Mr. Skatch was still making a struggling attempt to squeeze himself into the chimney. It was no use. That was clear enough. So, for the moment, Harry, the money box securely under his arm, felt safe.

Not for very long.

"If you don't come down instantly, I shall light the fires of Hell under you," the determined Mr. Skatch shouted.

Harry did not believe the colporteur would ever do such a thing. It would be too cruel. Too mean.

Too dreadful. So he stayed where he was, comfortably wedged in, merely peering down from time to time to see what in fact Mr. Skatch would do.

That gentleman pulled himself out of the fireplace and began to throw things into the hearth. Only then did Harry begin to think that perhaps Mr. Skatch *would* light a fire.

Frightened anew, Harry hastened up bit by bit, pausing only to take hasty glances down to see what was happening. He need not have bothered. Mr. Skatch was prepared to tell him.

"Throw the box down!" the colporteur hollered up the flue, "or I'll light the fire!"

To this demand Harry only climbed higher, scrambling as fast as he could, though he was beginning to feel it was not fast enough. Indeed, a smell of burning drifted up and eddied about.

Looking down, he saw Mr. Skatch holding a lit candle.

"Last chance!" cried that enlightened man.

Knees, elbows, hands and feet all pumped, pushing Harry up the inside of the chimney. He no longer dared take a second to look down.

"There!" called Mr. Skatch. "It's lit!"

The hot, dry smell of burning paper corkscrewed up the chimney, spinning about the air all around Harry's head. Clutching, pulling, the boy pushed up, tight fit though it was, till at last his fingers curled over the chimney top.

With one great heave and yank he hoisted his head into the open air.

Breathing freely, though at an understandably rapid rate, Harry waited only long enough to fill his lungs with fresh air. From below he was beginning to feel the heat become hotter and hotter.

Still holding the box, he dragged himself entirely up and out of the chimney, there to sit upon its wide stone top. Harry was quite on top of the house.

CHAPTER 36

NOT TO BE MISSED! · OUR ADVENTURE REACHES A VERY HIGH LEVEL INDEED

Harry *was* on top of the house. There is no question about that. On top. For the moment he was safe, though smoke and heat rose up from where he had just been. All things considered, he was greatly relieved to be where he was, sure that Mr. Skatch could never get him where he was at present placed.

Taking his moment's ease, Harry looked out over the countryside. Never had he seen it spread out so. Searching as far as he could, he hoped that he might see something, someone, who might help him. He could see the fields about the house and the woods that ran beyond. He could see the steeple of the distant Fairington church. He could even see the town itself. But there was no one to come, no one to help, no matter how far he looked.

Oh, how Harry wished he had wings! How far he would have flown. But even as he wished he berated himself for such foolish thoughts. He alone, he knew, had to decide what he could really do. Once more he looked about.

On the farthest side of the house, opposite where he was sitting, beyond the kitchen chimney, he saw the high branches of the great apple tree. If, he reasoned, he could reach those branches quickly, before Mr. Skatch could see what he was about, if he could do that, he would be able to climb down to the ground and run away.

But how was he to get to the other side? He considered straddling the rooftop and bumping himself across. That was a possibility, though it would take too much time. Worse, it might make too much noise and give him away.

The slate roof was perfectly smooth, with nothing to break a fall but the spikes that had been set up halfway down to keep winter snows from sliding. But on the topmost part of the roof, where the slanting sides of slate met, workmen had placed a thin *flat* strip all the way across.

It was four inches wide, perhaps half the height of this book. Just think!

Harry looked at this strip and wondered how quickly he could walk—or run—across it. That would be the fastest way to get across.

He put his hand over the chimney. Heat was still rising. So the only means of getting across and down quickly was to reach the apple tree. Moreover, he had to get there before Mr. Skatch saw what he meant to do.

Feeling a great sense of urgency, Harry made up his mind to go. On the instant, he rested one foot on the slate strip while remaining sitting on the chimney top. Off came his remaining shoe and both his socks. These he let slide down. With a thud they struck the ground.

Harry then pushed his left foot down on the slate strip, pressing down with all his weight.

The strip held firmly.

Slipping that foot forward, he swung his right foot behind and pressed that one down. All held steadily. He made himself stand up.

What was uppermost in his mind was that he had to hurry. That was the important thing.

So, setting the money box firmly under one arm, and holding the other arm out for balance, Harry began to slide his feet forward as he began to cross the roof.

Has there ever been such a book for lofty entertainment!

CHAPTER 37

A BRIEF INTERRUPTION DURING WHICH TIME WE RETURN TO MR. NARBUT, THE PYMS, AND SOME OTHERS WHO WERE PREVIOUSLY CONNECTED WITH THIS STORY, BUT WHOM WE MAY, IN OUR GREAT EXCITEMENT, HAVE FORGOTTEN

The very morning, the very hour, during which Harry was engaged in battle with Mr. Skatch at lofty levels, Mr. Seymour Narbut, constable of Fairington, made his way to the jail where he called out a low greeting to the Pyms.

"You'll be going before a judge this morning to make your guilty pleas," he informed them graciously. "Be ready when I come for you." And off he went.

Naturally, for Mr. Narbut was the most public of officials and believed in letting the citizens know what he was doing, he allowed word to go forth about the great event yet to come. Naturally there was quite a crowd of Fairingtonians gathered about the jail when it was time for the young people to meet the judge. They were there, of course, out of a simple desire to watch the great drama of law and order move to a happy conclusion, the people of the town being devoted to justice.

When Mr. Narbut returned to the jail after an ample breakfast, he chose his time carefully so that the greatest crowd of people would be there. He was smiling his best, swaggering and strutting as he took his place by the door.

"I'll bring 'em out right now," he informed his ardent admirers. "Don't let them get away," he warned with a wave.

The crowd cheered goodnaturedly to let him know that this would not happen.

In very short order Mr. Narbut returned to the street leading his two prisoners. Annie clung to Nicholas and Nicholas clung to Annie as both tried to stand proud against the press of the crowd. It was not an easy thing to do, and I'm afraid they were not able to bring it off. They rather cringed under the insults, jeers, and general caterwauling and did not make a very favorable impression. But then, they were frightened.

Among those looking on was the minister, Dr. Williams, who despite his grief could not keep away and looked sadly on, bewildered, not knowing what to think, much less what to do.

Down the street the throng moved, Mr. Narbut in the lead. Behind him came the Pyms; and all about them, like a great troop of clowns, came the folk who had come to watch, enjoy, and learn.

As they came, a coach, rattling and rolling, tumbled down the main street in a general confusion of dust and noise.

The coach had hardly stopped when one of the doors flew open, and who should leap out but Mr. Abraham Edgeworth himself, Harry's father. Mrs. Edgeworth, in an equal state of agitation, leaned out a window.

Seeing the crowd, seeing Mr. Narbut, seeing Miss Trowbridge—as the Edgeworths still knew her—Mr. Edgeworth called out: "Narbut! Narbut!" And in his hand he waved the very letter that the constable had sent him and that I am sure you had all but forgotten. You may be sure I didn't.

Mr. Narbut, at the head of the parade, saw his patron quickly enough and was only too glad to halt the mob. Here was yet the greatest opportunity to display his skill and sagacity.

"Ah, Mister Edgeworth," he cried. "How pleased I am to see you. Everything is under perfect control. Mistress Edgeworth! How do you do? Did you have a pleasant journey? I hope you did. Nothing to worry about at all. I assure you, your little boy is perfectly protected, at home with your dear and good friend Mr. Jeremiah Skatch."

Mr. Edgeworth, his side whiskers poking out in all directions, looked bewildered, which was only natural because he *was* bewildered. "Skatch?" he asked. "Who the devil is Skatch? My dear," he said to his equally puzzled wife, "do we have a dear and good friend by the name of Jeremiah Skatch?"

"No, of course not," said that lady, who knew their friends if her husband did not. "What's happened to Miss Trowbridge?" she demanded. "Why is she here? *What has happened to my darling boy?*"

"Now, now," Mr. Narbut began, trying to calm the Edgeworths in their great excitement. "I told you, *everything* is under control. Your small boy is with your friend Mister Skatch."

"Bunk and hornswoggle," roared Mr. Edgeworth, "I don't know who or what you are talking about. If she says I've no friend by the name of Skatch, I don't have one!"

"Don't you?" asked Mr. Narbut, his triumph beginning to wilt under the onslaught of the Edgeworths' response.

"Never heard of him in my life!" said Mr. Edgeworth.

It was left to Mrs. Edgeworth to remember. "Good God," she shrieked, though it was, to tell the truth, rather more of a scream, "that's the man we met in the coach, the one *you* talked to. What's he doing to my boy!"

Mr. Narbut stood for a moment, all eyes upon him. To give him credit—it is the only place I shall, so I had best do so at once—he grew palpably pale and said, "I think we had best get to your home."

Into the coach they all piled, the Edgeworths, Mr. Narbut, the Pyms, and somehow—this being *that* kind of a book—even Dr. Williams. We wouldn't want to leave him behind now, would we?

"Home!" cried Mr. Edgeworth out of the window.

"Where might that be?" returned the driver.

Mr. Edgeworth gave directions. The coach driver cracked his whip, enough of a crack to make any mere crack of dawn blush with envy.

Down the road the coach went, the horses plunging as if a race was to be run and they had every intention of winning it!

How little they knew of the true race that *was* being run.

CHAPTER 38

ALMOST A FINAL CHAPTER

Harry stood on the narrow strip of slate at the very top of the roof, one foot before the other. One arm was around the money box, while the other stretched out to keep him from falling and dashing out his brains.

He took a single step away from the protection of the chimney. It was not, to be truthful, so much a step as it was a slide. Nonetheless, it carried him forward. Drawing up his rear foot he slid that one forward. There he paused and took his breath, looking out over the glittering autumn gold of the world and the blue of the sky. He knew as he knew anything that he was altogether alone—nothing above and nothing below. He was himself alone.

He took another step.

"Damned fool!" rang out Mr. Skatch's voice from below. He had come out of the house in search of Harry and saw soon enough what the boy was doing. "Do you want to kill yourself?" he cried.

Harry's first impulse was to go back, but alas, that proved impossible. He could not turn. No, not even if he chose to. Nor did he even dare to look down at the colporteur. Instead, his eyes were fixed on the branches of the distant apple tree at the far, far, ever so far side of the house. All he wanted, with all his heart, soul, and mind, was to reach it.

Down below, Mr. Skatch, half crazed with frustration and anger, and desiring to divert the boy, began to shout out a song:

> *"There is a God that reigns above*
> *Lord of the heavens and ears and seas*
> *I fear his wrath, I ask his love*
> *And with my lips I sing his praise!"*

Harry tried to ignore this singing and instead took another step. It was there he wobbled (of course he wobbled—what would be the point of all this if he did not wobble?) and almost fell, his one arm waving wildly as he tried to find the proper balance. This swaying made him giddy.

(Of course it made him giddy!) His heart beat too fast. His very breath barely managed to squeeze itself in and out. Oh, if he could have gone back! Oh, if he could have just sat down and stayed where he was, he would have done so. *Gladly!* But really it *was* impossible. There was nothing for it but to go forward. Such is the fate of all who walk across a roof.

Below, Mr. Skatch continued singing, but now he switched to a mournful song:

> *"There is an hour when I must die*
> > *Nor do I know how soon 'twill come*
> *A thousand children young as I*
> > *Are call'd by death to hear their doom!"*

Each of Harry's little steps seemed to take him so long, but he took them all the same, one by one. Between each one of those steps he made certain of his place.

Mr. Skatch, chief protector of the Children's Protective Society, continued to sing:

> *"Let me improve the hours I have*
> > *Before the day of grace is fled*
> *There's no repentance in the grave*
> > *Nor pardon offer'd to the dead!"*

When Harry had gone about halfway across the

roof and saw that he was drawing closer to the tree, he began to feel very sure of himself. Instead of sliding his feet he sought to walk. It was—but you've already guessed—a mistake.

He began to sway, he started to fall. Quickly he managed to get himself into a squat, holding the box out far to one side, his one free hand to the other. It steadied him.

Then slowly, oh, so *very* slowly, he rose up again and returned to his more carefully measured sliding steps.

Below, Mr. Skatch, quite beside himself, continued to sing:

> "*Just as the tree cut down, that fell*
>   *To North or Southward, there it lies*
> *So man departs to heaven or hell*
>   *Fix'd in the state wherein he dies!*"

Onward Harry continued, the arms of the apple tree seeming to beckon, implore, pull at him. Those branches of the tree were all he saw in the world. He even had visions of those branches growing longer, larger, reaching toward him, taking hold of him. Though he didn't want to go fast again, he found himself moving quicker, always quicker, all but falling forward, not actually running, till at last he flung himself at the kitchen chimney!

He began to sway, he started to fall.

It seemed to Harry to be the most solid thing in all creation. A chimney!

CHAPTER 39

THE VERY LAST CHAPTER BEFORE THE FINAL CHAPTER

Now that he was leaning against the chimney, Harry felt much safer than before. Decidedly so. But that did not mean that he was free of Mr. Skatch. No. That determined gentleman was still standing below, watching every move the boy made, even as Harry, money box in his lap, rested against the chimney.

"You're the Devil's own!" cried the colporteur (who should have known, if anyone did), his patience all gone. "I should have seen from the first! I might have just come and taken the bloody box from you. But I was kind to you. Do you hear me," he screamed at the top of his voice from the bottom of his hate-filled soul, "I was kind!"

Harry, reverting to his usual practice, did nothing but look at the man.

"Look here," bellowed Mr. Skatch. "Even a

man as patient as I can wait only so long. Will you or won't you come down?"

Instead of answering, Harry reached into the branches of the tree and plucked himself an apple.

There was something about that simple gesture of picking an apple that brought Mr. Skatch's rage to a total boil. "Didn't you hear me, you impudent, worthless, useless child!" And reaching into his pocket, he drew forth his loaded pistol. "Do you see *this!*" he screamed, pointing the gun right at Harry. "Do you?"

Harry, who had indeed seen the gun, rose up in his place.

"It's no sin to destroy sin!" ranted Mr. Skatch. "And you're the worst of the worst! Look at you, with an apple in your hand. An apple like they ate at Eden! I give you this last time to throw down that box! By God, I'll shoot you if you don't. Don't you see, I've had enough: *I want that money!*"

Harry, standing transfixed, only stared at him, apple in one hand, box in the other.

"Last warning!" cried Mr. Skatch. "Last absolute and only warning! I shall count to ten. If you don't throw that box down, you'll be the one to make me pull this trigger, and I say—the Devil take you!"

Harry eyed the tree, wondering if it were possible for him to leap behind its branches for protection.

"One—two—" began Mr. Skatch.

With a sudden motion, Harry cocked back his arm, and hurled the apple he had been holding straight at Mr. Skatch. The apple, flying as true as Harry ever threw, struck the colporteur squarely upon the forehead.

Down Mr. Skatch crumpled into a stunned heap as the pistol, flying into the air, fired harmlessly.

Instantly, Harry reached for the nearest branch, and with the speed of a stone coming home to earth, slipped to the ground. Once there he ran to where the pistol lay and picked it up.

In fact, he was standing there, pistol in hand, not very far from the unconscious Mr. Skatch, trying to decide what to do next, when the coach tore down upon him out of the woods. In moments the Edgeworths' small boy was surrounded by the major characters of this book: his mother, his father, the Pyms, Dr. Williams, and of course, Constable Seymour Narbut.

CHAPTER 40

AT LAST! THE FINAL CHAPTER!

Harry told the entire story quickly enough, and I don't doubt but that he told it much faster than I've told it here.

"There!" cried Mr. Narbut, who had busied himself tying the hands and feet of Mr. Skatch. "Didn't I say trouble would come? Didn't I say I would protect the boy? Didn't things work out just dandy? Smoke out the real thief. That's the only way. I knew all along this Skatch was nothing of what he said. But you need proof, solid proof. Yes, I'm a silent mover."

"Horatio, dearest boy," said Mr. Edgeworth, who, ignoring the constable, was kneeling on the ground so he could look his boy squarely in the face, "what kind of parents do you think you have? Do you think I'd ever want you to worry about such a thing as my money?" So saying, he scooped the money box away from Harry and pulled it open.

"Look here," boomed Mr. Edgeworth, showing Harry the inside of the box. "I put all the money in the bank before I left! There's nothing here but one fifty-cent piece."

"Nothing there?" said Mrs. Edgeworth, thoroughly surprised.

"Nothing there?" said Mr. Narbut, growing red in the face.

"Nothing there?" said Dr. Williams in bewilderment.

"Nothing there?" said Mrs. Pym, growing angry.

"Nothing there?" said Mr. Pym in amazement.

"Nothing there?" said Mr. Skatch with a dreadful oath that nobody should listen to.

"*Nothing there?*" whispered Harry, hardly believing what he could see very well for himself.

"Of course not," said Mr. Edgeworth, almost chiding the boy. "Do you think I'd be so unfeeling as to even think of giving such a responsibility to a small boy like you? Precious Horatio, my job is to *protect* you!"

For a terrible moment Harry felt that he was back on the roof. But when he caught his breath, he turned about till he faced Mrs. Pym. "I am truly sorry that I wronged you, ma'am," he said, going to her. "But you wouldn't tell me who he was."

Mrs. Pym could only nod.

Harry next turned to Mr. Pym. "I'm sorry, too, about you, sir. But I didn't know who you really were."

"Guess so," admitted that young man with a pull to his nose.

Harry next turned to Mr. Narbut, but the constable didn't give the boy a chance. "Don't have to apologize to me, my boy," he said. "I had it all planned out."

Harry looked about. He saw Mr. Skatch, his once brilliant face reduced to a black hole. He saw his father and his mother looking at him with tender mercy in their eyes. He saw Dr. Williams with a tearful, toothless but nonetheless happy smile. He saw the Pyms. And they were all looking at him—looking at him *exactly* the same way, with sentimental pity. And he knew that they saw him as small and delicate, as if he couldn't take care of himself.

Harry considered these looks, shrugged, turned about, and started to walk off.

"Horatio Stockton Edgeworth!" cried Mrs. Edgeworth, alarmed. "Where are you going?"

"To take a walk," returned Harry over his shoulder.

"Dear boy," called Mr. Edgeworth. "You've not had your breakfast."

"Don't wait for me," announced Harry as he continued, hands in pockets, to move on. "I can take care of myself."

. . . they were all looking at him—looking at him **exactly**
the same way . . .

I guess he did, too, because that marked the end of the Children's Protective Society—at least in Fairington. Of course, I don't know about *your* neighborhood. That might be another story all over again.

Do let me know.

AVI is an award-winning author of over two dozen books for young people. Among these are the Newbery Honor Books *The True Confessions of Charlotte Doyle* and *Nothing but the Truth*; *The Fighting Ground*, winner of the Scott O'Dell Award for Historical Fiction; *Wolf Rider*, an ALA *Booklist* Best Book of the 1980s; *Captain Grey; Smugglers' Island; Man from the Sky; Emily Upham's Revenge; Night Journeys*; and *Encounter at Easton*. He lives in Providence, Rhode Island.

PAUL O. ZELINSKY, a two-time Caldecott Honor artist for *Rumplestiltskin* and *Hansel and Gretel*, also illustrated Avi's *Emily Upham's Revenge*. He lives in Brooklyn, New York.